LYNNE WAITE CHAPMAN

Secret Guilt
Small Town Mystery, Book 1
By Lynne Waite Chapman

Copyright © 2022 by Lynne Waite Chapman

Published by Gordian Books, an imprint of Winged Publications

Cover design by Cynthia Hickey

This book is a work of fiction. Names, characters, places, and incidents are the product of the author's imagination and are used fictitiously. Any resemblance to actual events, locales, or persons, living or dead, is coincidental.

All rights reserved including the right to reproduce this book or portions thereof in any form whatsoever – except short passages for reviews – without express permission.

ISBN: 979-8-8690-8015-8

Chapter One

"Mom? Is that you?" I shouted above the noise of water rushing into the sink, then pushed down the lever. The hot water slammed against the shut off valve with a thump. Listening for a moment, I waited for a repeat of the noise from the foyer. Nothing.

I'd been cleaning the sink while lost in a daydream. Thinking I'd like to take a road trip. A mini-vacation. Maybe a trip to the ocean. A drive down to see the leaves change color in southern Indiana would be closer to fitting my budget. Before my thoughts were interrupted, I'd been balancing the feel of sand in my toes to the earthy scent of the woodland trails in Brown County State Park.

Back to reality. I turned my head so one ear was pointed toward the hallway. As a child I'd always imagined I could hear better that way. My mother, if it was her in the foyer, was being extraordinarily quiet. But who else would it be?

I tossed the rag into the sink and then gathered the leftovers from the counter to store in the refrigerator. I raised my voice a notch and called out once again.

"Mom, I thought this was your day at the church food pantry."

No answer. I stood still, slowed my breathing, listening.

Okay, pretty sure I hadn't imagined the noise at the front door. It was most certainly my mother. Who else would walk into my house unannounced? Even my closest friends tapped on the door and called my name before barging in.

My mother, on the other hand, wouldn't see the need for knocking. I'd learned not to expect privacy when it came to Katherine Cassell. After all, this used to be her house. I bought the comfortable Craftsman style bungalow when she relocated to Clairmont Retirement Village. With the swipe of a pen, the name on the mortgage changed from Katherine Baron Cassell to Liberty Breeze Cassell, sealing a bargain for both of us. I couldn't turn down the deal on a house, and she was happy that the home where she'd raised her family wouldn't be trampled on by strangers.

With carrots in my hand, ready to toss into the crisper, I glanced over my shoulder toward the hallway that led to the front door. Still no answer, save a slight creak of the old wooden floor. The aging house settling. All was quiet at the moment, but I couldn't shake the certainty that I'd heard something. Though not the familiar clippity-clip of Mom's size four pumps. Not to mention the running update on her morning activities. It was her habit to begin commentary the moment she stepped inside and continue it until well after she'd found me in whatever room I happened to be in.

I stood in the silent kitchen, waiting. And if I'm honest, growing impatient. There were chores to be done, a schedule to keep. I had a job to get to. My mother thought she was busy, but it was all volunteer work.

Maybe it wasn't her after all. "Clair, is that you?" No, my friend Clair would have made herself known by now. She was seldom still. Always running to appointments to build her new real estate business. If not that, she would be helping her husband in his veterinary clinic.

It must be my mother. Knowing her, she'd been distracted by the dust on my entry table or maybe she'd stepped in and felt the need to rearrange the books on my shelf. Honestly, she wore me out sometimes.

I took two steps and glanced down the hallway. I needed to finish cleaning the kitchen and get on my way to work, but this intrusion called for further investigation.

If it was my mother, and I was certain of that, she'd gotten sidetracked. Maybe admiring the vase of sunflowers I'd placed by the front door. I'd made an early trip to the farmers market and the huge blossoms created a splash of color on my entry table. If she was so enamored with it, I'd send it home with her.

I took a deep breath to stifle an angry outburst. On the whole, I'm a patient person, but was fast becoming frustrated. What was that woman doing? I stepped back into the kitchen and tossed the carrots into the refrigerator. With fists planted on my hips, I called again. "Katherine Cassell, answer me before I freak out and grab the shotgun."

Okay, that was a joke. Ours was a peace-loving family. I'd never owned a firearm, shotgun or otherwise. My mother would grow faint if I even mentioned getting one. No taser or pepper spray either.

Still no answer to my calls. With a puff of breath, I

started down the hall to where I assumed she would be standing. Then I heard something not at all familiar. Heavy treads retreating. Out through the entry and across the threshold and wooden porch. Then down the front steps to the sidewalk. By the time I'd reached the door and leaned out, there was nothing to see. A rustle in the thick forsythia bushes along the side of the house, but nothing my straining eyes could pick out.

"I did not imagine it. Now I'm certain there was someone in here." I spoke to the walls. Living alone, I often feel the need to reassure myself, out loud. Doesn't everyone? Or was it the sneaky approach of middle age?

I mentally sorted through possible explanations for the intrusion until I came up with the wandering elderly neighbor possibility. One of the aging residents on the block had mistakenly entered my house. They would have been really embarrassed at the gaffe. If it had been me, I would have sneaked out and taken off running, too.

I took one last peek outside. A beautiful morning. Sun shining and leaves just beginning to turn. The breeze brought in a whiff of smoke. Someone had already lit their fireplace or firepit.

I shuffled inside for a glance into the living room. "Helloooo. Anyone in here?" No answer. No one there. I returned to the kitchen and hustled to finish the morning cleanup.

I could write about this in my journal. An exciting day in a small town.

~~

The clock clicked past nine a.m. And I gathered my handbag and a sweater, pulling the door shut on my way out. Couldn't have asked for a nicer day to walk to work. We wouldn't be blessed with this beautiful fall weather forever. Sunshine warm on my face and cool breezes ruffling my hair, enough to put the weirdness of the morning out of my mind. But as I reached the sidewalk, I paused to check out the yard and shrubs around the house. Nothing suspicious. Everything as it should be.

Had I locked the door? I wasn't always careful. It was so easy to be lax about security in a neighborhood where you knew all of the neighbors by name. First house on the right, Ron and Linda Charrigan, empty nesters. Not much activity there since the twins left home. Next to them was a fairly new couple, Dale and Sharon something, busy most of the time. I only saw them when they returned from work and disappeared inside. The next was Mr. Lester. I had no idea what his first name was. Maybe Oscar? He was old enough to warrant formality.

I quit trying to remember names for the rest of the block. There had been a few changes over the years. I guess I didn't know everyone as well as I'd thought. Though even without remembering their names, I recognized faces. I trusted my neighbors. If any of them walked into my house without invitation, it had been an accident.

I put the morning's excitement behind me and continued the three-block trek to Bennett's Hardware, where I served as bookkeeper, sometimes clerk, sometimes cleaning lady.

I took my time strolling down the block. Working for Stanley Bennett didn't require a time clock. I was the only employee, except for Jimmy Conklin, a high school senior, who worked a few hours on weekends. The boss relied on my work ethic, and I tried to maintain that trust. Keeping the books for the little store was easy—no stress. Didn't take much of my time. It didn't pay much either, but the paycheck covered expenses, which I managed to keep to a minimum. I wasn't about to spend life working myself to death in order to buy a lot of things. Live simple, enjoy life. That was my motto.

I scanned the window display as I arrived. Maybe I'd suggest Mr. Bennett call the window washer. My cramped little office was located behind the sales counter. I loved the familiar scent. Leather, old wood, and used books. And dust, if I was honest. The room held a sense of history, and of stability. I took my place at the ancient wooden desk, easing into the equally ancient, worn leather chair.

Mr. Bennett appeared at the door and leaned in to say hello while I booted up the computer. "Did you see the game Friday night? This is going to be a good year for our team."

"No. But I heard it was a good one, Mr. Bennett. I spent the afternoon trimming bushes and was too tired to go." Everyone in town called him Stanley, but my mother had coached me to be formal since he was my elder and my boss. And he never objected.

"I noticed that you walked to work today. Car problems?"

"No. The car's fine. I felt like walking."

"I'll give you a ride home. Just let me know when you're finished."

"Thanks Mr. Bennett, but there's no need for a ride. I'm looking forward to the walk. It's beautiful out there."

"Might rain."

Stifling a sigh, I thought of dear Mr. Bennett. He was a nice man and sounded just like my mother. I secretly thought the two would make a good couple. But I had no clue as to how to kick-start that relationship. They both seemed happy being single. "I don't believe there's any precipitation in the forecast, but thanks for the offer." My boss had already walked back into the sales floor.

I sorted the previous day's receipts and stacked them in a neat pile on my desk. Before continuing, I made a trip to the coffee pot. Mr. Bennett had the same idea. He poured a second cup and handed it to me.

I knew he liked hearing comments on the business. "Sales picked up last month, Mr. Bennett. There was a nice uptick in activity over the last couple weeks. More than enough to pay for the new shelving."

This produced a wide grin and a nod. "I thought I noticed an increase in business, Libby. Good to know the books confirm it."

Mr. Bennett carried his coffee to the counter to study his clipboard. I returned to the office to finish recording sales.

I noticed he stood, coffee in hand, for an unusual amount of time. He seemed fixated on the front window. I expected to hear a customer arrive, but Mr. Bennett whirled around to face me. "By the way, I haven't seen your mother lately. How is she?"

Recent concerns about my mother's wellbeing confirmed my thinking the man might have a crush on her. He simply hadn't worked up the courage to pursue it. With further consideration, I wavered between wanting to encourage the relationship and the desire to run for cover. They could both use the companionship. But then, he was my boss. How often did I really want to see him? Holidays? Sunday dinners?

I guessed Stanley Bennett to be a little younger than my mother. Possibly sixty-five or so, although he never spoke of retiring. Hair thinning enough to see scalp shining through. Glasses with frames old enough to have gone out of style and back in again. He was a dependable man, and predictable. Always wore gray slacks and a white shirt. Short or long sleeved, depending on the season. He never wore jeans and never sneakers. Very much the gentleman pictured in the old movies my mother watched.

"She's well. You know Mom. She keeps busy taking care of the community. The food pantry and clothing drives. Last week she volunteered to take a turn at delivering meals to the home bound."

Stanley's eyes sparkled. "Katherine's a gem. What would Twin Fawn do without her?" He paused for a moment. "I suppose the volunteer work helps since she's alone. Does she have, um, a gentleman friend?"

I clamped my mouth shut to stifle the laugh. A gentleman friend? Not that my mother wasn't attractive enough to have a boyfriend. She dressed nice and wasn't any more overweight than most women in their late sixties. Mr. Bennett's question might have come from a nervous schoolboy. "I haven't noticed anyone vying for her attention if that's what you're asking. She's so focused on her charities a man would have to be particularly determined to spend time with her."

"Hmm." Mr. Bennett picked up his clipboard and returned to checking in new deliveries.

I dropped the stack of receipts and picked up my coffee. I'd have to mull this one over. He was nice enough, but Stanley Bennett as a stepfather? I reminded myself to slow down. What was I thinking? They were old. If they dated, it would mean companionship. That's all.

I re-stacked the papers and focused on my work.

Later, as I pulled out my lunch bag, earlier events of the morning came to mind prompting a call to my mother. "Did you stop by the house this morning?"

Her voice, cheerful as always, bubbled through the line. "No. Was I supposed to?"

"Well, I didn't expect you, but I thought I heard you at the door. You know, like you might have stopped in and then changed your mind. Maybe turned around and left before coming in?"

She chuckled. "I spent the morning at the food pantry. You know it's my morning to serve. And if I'd been to the house, I certainly wouldn't have left without talking to you."

"It does sound silly, now that I put it into words. But I heard someone come in. I didn't get an answer when I called out. Then, a couple minutes later I heard them leave."

"That's strange. Are you positive you heard it?"

"Yes, Mother. I'm sure." Sort of sure.

"Didn't you go to the door to see who it was?"

"Of course, I did. Not right away because I was getting ready to go to work. And I thought it was you. When I decided to investigate, whoever it was must have heard me and left."

I couldn't help myself. I felt the need to ask again. "Think back. Are you certain you didn't stop in this morning?"

"I just told you I wasn't there. Do I make a habit of sneaking into your house and then running away? That's a child's stunt."

"Of course, you don't. Sorry. I didn't mean to insult you. Just covering all the bases." A child's stunt or my aging mother's forgetfulness?

I took a minute to chew a carrot stick. "I know it wasn't you. It was weird, though. Maybe it was a mistake. Do you know if any of the older people in the neighborhood have been getting confused? You know, wandering?"

"No Dear, I'm sure I don't know of anyone." She paused. "But that is a worry. There are a few who are getting along in years. Willow Ottenweller is only in her seventies but aging, if you know what I mean. And there's Lorin Sanderson who lives on the next block. He seems to be doing okay but must be ninety by now."

I heard a couple of deep breaths come through the line and she hummed a note before continuing. "I think I'll call a few of the people in the neighborhood, just to check on them. Someone could have had a stroke that affected their memory. So dangerous. I'd hate to think they might wander away and not be able to find their way home. I'm going to start calling right now. I won't be able to rest until I know."

Oh shoot. My mother kept herself busy enough, and now I'd given her another mission. When would I learn to be careful what I shared with her? "Please don't stew over this. You take care of enough people. There's no need to go looking for more. It could have been anyone. Even Roy from across the street. Could have had his mind on something and walked up the wrong sidewalk."

"Maybe." I hoped I detected a touch of relief in her voice. "You know, I've done that myself. Last week I tried to get in the wrong car. It was almost the same color as mine. I'd started to climb in before I noticed there were bags in the back seat and they didn't belong to me." She chuckled. "Okay. I'll check around. But I won't lose sleep over it."

"Good. I'll let you go. Have to get back to work." As I thought about it, I was pretty sure she would lose sleep over it. I crushed the brown paper bag and tossed it in the waste can.

Five minutes later, the phone rang. "Will I see you at church on Sunday?"

"Of course. I'll be there, Mom. When have you not seen me at church on Sunday morning?" I sat with her every week, front row, same place. Center aisle. Fourth seat from the right."

"Yes, Liberty. You are always faithful. I don't want you to think I take it for granted. I appreciate you. Have a nice day."

"Bye, Mom." I sat and mulled over the name my parents gave me. Liberty. At least she hadn't used my middle name as well. Breeze. What kind of name was that? It gave the impression I'd been brought up in a commune. People might think that my parents were a couple of hippies. Nothing could be farther from the truth. There had never been any bohemian tendencies in my family.

My father served at the Twin Fawn post office for twenty-five years, before suffering a massive heart attack. My mother couldn't have been any more conservative. Who or what had convinced my parents to name me Liberty Breeze, I couldn't figure. They grew up in the sixties but certainly never would have been caught protesting the establishment. Not a rebellious bone in either of them.

I grew up following behind her, telling everyone to call me Libby, or maybe Lib. Whenever anyone asked me what Libby was short for, I'd tell them Elisabeth, unless of course my parents were within earshot. My mother insisted on calling me Liberty and sometimes Liberty Breeze.

Other than exhibiting strange taste in naming her only daughter, my mother was perfect. A saint. She would never utter a cuss word or even raise her voice in anger. Kindest and sweetest woman who ever lived. If she had any flaw, it might be that she never thought of herself, always too busy helping others. She jumped in to work every charity project. People loved her. Everyone in town knew they could depend on Katherine Cassell. She would supply meals, clean a house, sit with the elderly. The woman should be given an award.

Later in the afternoon I answered the phone. My mother on the line, again. "Liberty, I did some checking on the neighbors. No one admitted to walking into the house. I think they would have told me if they had. You know the people in the neighborhood are very honest. I bet what you heard was noise from the television. Was it on in the other room? That was probably it. I know as well as anyone how living alone can cause a person to imagine things. Well dear, I have to run."

"I didn't imagine it." Too late to protest my sanity. She had already clicked off.

If not an elderly neighbor, then who? And, it was not just television noise. The set had been off. One thing was certain. I'd heard footsteps. And that meant only one thing.

Whether by accident of on purpose someone had been in my house.

Chapter Two

"Mr. Bennett, the filing is finished. What else can I do for you?" Two or three hours in the office was cozy. More than that turned claustrophobic. "Why don't you let me help you put out new inventory?"

Resting a hand on his lower back, the boss straightened. "You know, Libby, that's a good idea. If you would be good enough to stock the shelves, I could run to the bank. I have a few more errands I might take care of, too."

Wait. How long would that take? Did I say I wanted to run the store? I would have been happy playing stockboy. There was little stress in organizing shelves. But I never wanted to be in charge. I didn't enjoy running the cash register.

Mr. Bennett wasted no time in removing his work apron. "It'll only take me a couple hours."

Looked like I'd volunteered for a new job description.

He leaned against the counter and folded the apron. "We received the nail shipment yesterday. Two and a half inch stainless steels. You'll find it stacked in the back room. There are a lot of them, but they're boxed, only 350 in each. Perfect size for the do-it-yourselfer. "

He pointed to the back corner of the store and lifted his chin to gaze over the closer shelves. "You know those wide shelves in the corner? There's a lot of wasted space there. You can begin stacking the boxes from the back. Shove them as far in as possible and fill to the front. Then, as they sell, we can pull them forward."

"Let me take a look before you go to make sure I get the right thing." I made the trip to the storeroom and came up against stacks of boxes. "Wow. When did those come in? You really stocked up." There must have been a hundred boxes.

Mr. Bennett's eyes lit up. Anyone would have thought he was showing off a new puppy. "I got a great buy. They were delivered last night. And you know they will always sell. Nails aren't about to go out of style, are they?"

I chuckled. He sounded like my friend Clair at a shoe sale. She never found a reason to pass up a new pair of heels. "I guess not. No sense missing out on a bargain."

My boss left the store, and I went in search of the dolly. Stacking it with boxes, I decided I could skip my gym workout. Just kidding. I hadn't set foot in a gym for months and needed no excuse to avoid it. After I'd loaded what I could handle, I transferred the cargo from the storeroom to the sales floor.

After thirty minutes of squatting to shove the small boxes to the back of the shelf, muscles in my legs threatened to lock in that position. The floor didn't seem excessively dirty. Jimmy must have swept on the weekend. I sat on the floor, stretched my legs, and breathed relief.

I threw myself into my work and had practically crawled into the lowest opening. My arm was extended deep into the shelving, when a shadow fell across me. A scent of smoke and sweat wafted past. From the corner of my eye, I could see massive work boots on the floor next to me.

Startled, I pulled myself from inside the unit, and banged my head on the way out. "Oh. Hi. Sorry, I didn't hear you come in."

I grabbed the edge of a shelf and struggled to my feet, sizing up the customer as I stood. The aforementioned boots-size large, jeans-not new, work shirt-worn. Finally, an untrimmed beard and dark hair heavily dusted with gray. I brushed off my hands on my pants. "I didn't mean to ignore you. Can't hear much under there. How can I help you?"

The man's dark expressionless eyes roamed me from head to toe. I stared back, heart rate picking up and mind working out the fastest escape route from the store, if an escape became necessary.

When he finally spoke, it was with a deep gruff voice much like a villain in Clair's favorite suspense flicks. "Yeah. I was beginning to think no one was here."

I had to tip my head back to look at the customer's face. He didn't seem to have any concept of personal space. I stood alone with this strange man in the store. When did Mr. Bennett say he would be back? Was there a weapon within reach? I shot a glance at a box of nails I'd left on the top shelf.

All the while I planned my defense, guilt niggled at the back of my mind. I didn't know this man. Why did I assume he was a threat? It was wrong to think poorly of him simply because he didn't fit the image of a clean-cut Twin Fawn resident. Most likely he would seem perfectly respectable if someone suggested he get a haircut and beard trim. And a change of clothes. Not me. Someone else. Maybe his wife?

My mother's words came to mind. "Never make a snap judgement by a person's appearance. You don't know what's in his heart."

The man smiled, displaying yellowed teeth, but all the same, improving his appearance. "I'm looking for a few tools to fix up an old house I'm renting."

A wreck of a house came to mind. A shack that probably should have been torn down years ago. All the other houses on the street were in decent shape and were occupied. "Oh, is it the one on Elm?"

"Ah, no. It's farmhouse way out in the country. I need a few things for repairs."

Oops. Why did I insist on jumping to conclusions? "Oh, sure. I'm positive we have what you need. You'll find we stock a little bit of everything. The owner isn't here right now, but I'll help if I can. I'm the bookkeeper." Shoot. Was that too much detail? Clair had always accused me of offering too much information. Her reproach came to mind. "TMI, Libby, TMI!" Why did I blurt out, to this stranger, I was alone in the store?

"I see you've already found the shopping basket." Fingers that gripped the handle were nicotine stained.

"Just take your time and look around. You'll find what you need."

I heard a familiar creak and glanced in the direction of the squeaky front door. It was my mother. She stood in the doorway, brought a hand to her chin and muttered something I couldn't hear. Then the woman turned and practically ran back to the street, letting the door bang shut.

For once, I would have been happy for her bursting

in. But what had gotten into her? She didn't even say hello, but acted as if she didn't know me. She might have been my only hope. Didn't she see I was alone with a scary stranger?

I dragged my attention back to the disheveled man in front of me. He hadn't moved but was still staring at me. I'd never been one of those girls that men couldn't take their eyes off. This guy made me jumpier by the minute.

Where was Mr. Bennett? Shouldn't he be back by now? I sent up an arrow-prayer for more customers to descend on the hardware store.

I subtly slid back a step. The space between the shelving unit and the wall was already cramped and the walls were closing in fast. Not sure how I could put more distance between us without being obvious.

"Um. Is there something I can help you find?"

All I got was a slight shake of his head. "No. I thought I knew you, but it's nothin'."

The door of the store banged open again and I flinched as if I'd been shot. I gulped a breath and scanned the front of the store in search of my rescuer.

Garret Reed strode in, saw me by the wall and started my way. Tall. Dark wavy hair. Big smile bracketed by the cutest dimples. "Hey Libby, how's it going?"

I wanted to laugh and could have hugged him. All thoughts of mayhem evaporated. "Hi, Garrett. It's so good to see you. What are you up to today?" I'd tried for casual, but did I sound desperate?

I frantically searched my brain for conversation. Anything to keep Garret in the store until Big Foot left. "What can I help you with?"

"I'm looking for a hammer. It's crazy. I've had mine for like twenty years and now I can't find it. Don't know when it disappeared. It could have been months ago. I don't have many occasions to use it." He flashed a lopsided smile. "Anyway, I need one now."

"We have a display up next to the window. All shapes and sizes. Let me show you." I sidestepped down the aisle, away from Big Foot. Very aware I was behaving like an idiot. Mr. Bennett did not see the need for all shapes and sizes of anything. We might have had more than one style hammer, but I doubted it.

Garret glanced in the direction of the display. "I see it. You're busy. There's no need for you to bother showing me." He began to walk. I began to panic.

"No bother." I reached the end of the aisle, slid out and tagged along, leaving Big Foot behind. It was rude, but fear usually trumps manners for me.

I stood behind Garrett while he weighed the difference between our selection of two hammers. One with a red grip. One with black. How could I keep him in the store until after Big Foot left?

I glanced over my shoulder. My other customer had filled his basket and made his way to the cash register. I watched as he placed his selections on the counter. Yes! Garrett would have to wait.

I scooted up and did my best to be friendly, easier now that Garrett was in the store. "Did you find everything you were looking for?" I began ringing up his purchases as fast as my fingers could punch in the numbers.

The big man glanced at Garret and back at me. "I guess I have enough." I bagged his items, my eyes looking everywhere but at him.

With a dip of the chin, almost a bow, he said, "Thank you, miss." I took a mental step back. How sweet. Sort of an old-fashioned tip of the hat to a lady. Maybe I'd jumped to conclusions about this stranger. I'd been suspicious and unwelcoming, simply because of his appearance. Still, his appearance made me uneasy.

The man exited Bennett's Hardware, and Garret approached the counter. Tall dark and handsome. He'd grown up well. The perfect hero for any love story. I'd had a crush on him since I was in the third grade, and he was in fifth.

I breathed relief and gushed like a six-year-old. "Is there anything else?"

"Nope. I decided I could use a screwdriver, too.

He placed his two items on the counter. Picture me, the adoring schoolgirl staring at my knight in shining armor. He'd rescued me from a dangerous situation. Maybe only in my imagination. But imagination or not, a hero was still a hero.

"Are you feeling okay? You look a little flushed."

"Do I?" Was it from the encounter with Big Foot or from standing so close to Garrett? "It was a little warm over there where I was stocking shelves. That must have been it."

I gazed into those chocolate brown eyes, very similar to Big Foot's dark eyes, but with warmth that invited me in.

Garrett glanced down at his hand. I followed his gaze and saw that he was holding cash.

Cash, yes, cash. Focus on the task and not the hero's eyes. And certainly, not on the creepy do-it-yourselfer.

Chapter Three

After some effort convincing Mr. Bennett that I liked to walk—and resorting to the lie that my doctor had urged me to get more exercise—I strolled the peaceful streets of Twin Fawn on my way home. It was a rare occasion when I had something interesting to share with my friend Clair. On this exceptional day I pulled out my cell phone to punch in her number. Since she and her husband Michael had moved to Twin Fawn, she had been the voice of logic to my slightly hysterical emotional thoughts.

Before I could hit the first number, the phone rang, and I swiped to answer. "Great minds. I had my hand on the phone to call you. Isn't that weird?" It was a rhetorical question. "Speaking of weird, you have to hear what happened to me at work, today." I paused only long enough to check for traffic while crossing a street. "Now that I think about it, I may have judged it all wrong. You know how my imagination gets away from me sometimes. Anyway, this customer, I'll call him Big Foot, 'cause I didn't get his name and the first thing I noticed was how large his feet were. I know it isn't very nice of me but that's what pops to mind when I think of him." I described the incident, adding details as they came to mind and embellishing on my first impressions.

"Do you think I'm crazy? Maybe he was just a regular guy. Probably was, but you know me. My mind exploded with all kinds of crazy scenarios." Why did I do that? There were times I couldn't help making up things to worry about. "But he looked sort of frightening. The kind of scary that you see on the nightly news when they arrest an ax murderer."

My friend, Clair, listened politely, which was not always her strong point. But she jumped in when I paused to breathe.

"Do you really think a criminal walked into the store? Could it have been an unfortunately awkward man? Have you looked around town? There are plenty of guys who need a shave and a shower. If he'd been working, restoring the farmhouse, his clothes would have been dirty. And the man has no control over the size of his feet."

I gulped. "I see your point. Geesh. I got worked up over nothing. I should be ashamed of myself. Darn, what I should have done is ask him his name and welcome him to Twin Fawn. If I'd been sane... If I had been you, or my mother, I would have."

My friend, the voice of encouragement, knew the right words. "Don't be hard on yourself. In real estate, I'm used to talking to all kinds of people, so I don't get rattled. And we all know your mother would welcome that ax murderer to town while trying to save his soul."

I laughed. "You're right, she would."

I stopped to sit on a bench in Bird Song Park, a little rest area the town had provided in the middle of the block. It served no purpose other than the enjoyment of citizens of Twin Fawn. "If I see the man again, I'll make extra effort to be friendly. Maybe I'll inquire about how he's progressing on the house and if he's getting settled. I can be welcoming, too."

"See how you've talked yourself out of being scared of him. I'm glad you called."

"Me too." I leaned back on the bench and watched a squirrel scamper up a tree. "Wait. You called me. What did you want?"

Silence on the phone. "I don't remember. It must not have been important. When it comes back to me, I'll call you."

The squirrel jumped to the ground and ran off. "Wait, don't hang up. I haven't told you the best part. You have to hear how I was rescued from Beg Foot's threat, however imaginary."

I inserted a pause for effect. A short pause because excitement bubbled up and I couldn't keep quiet.

"It turned out that I wasn't alone in the store with Big Foot for very long. Another customer came into the store while he shopped."

"Oh, good. I'm sure that made you feel safer."

"And it wasn't just any old customer. You'll never guess who it was."

"You're right. I won't, so tell me. You know I hate guessing games."

"Tall. Dark. Some might say smoldering." I knew Clair would grow impatient if I continued with the clues. "Sorry. It was Garrett Reed! Garrett Reed walked into the store." I said his name through a big smile that I'm certain Clair could detect.

"Wow! Now that's what I call good timing. Nothing like a good-looking man to take your mind off your troubles."

I was quiet, reliving the few minutes Garrett had been near me.

"So, with Big Foot gone, you and Garrett were alone in the store. What did you talk about?"

"Nothing. I rang up his order and he left." I sighed. "You know I couldn't have come up with witty banter when that man stood less than two feet from me."

"If I wasn't married, I'd have been tongue-tied, too." No, she wouldn't. Clair never found herself tongue-tied. Very nice of her to encourage me.

We ended our call with a promise to talk later. I continued the walk home with pleasant thoughts and a smile on my face. Big Foot, the imaginary monster, forgotten. My hero, Garrett, front and center.

As I got closer to my house, I remembered there was actually someone to worry about. My dear mother might be showing her age. How could I explain her odd behavior? I would swear she'd almost come into the hardware store but then, left. Why did she suddenly change her mind? Even though she'd denied it, I suspected she had done the same at my house that morning. My mother wouldn't lie, but was it possible she didn't even remember? Short term memory loss happens to people of a certain age. There's a point when children find themselves looking to the welfare of the parent.

She answered at the first ring. "Hey, Mom. So, what happened to you at the store?"

"I'm sorry, Liberty. I don't know what you mean. What store?"

That confirmed it. She was losing her mind.

I spoke slowly, enunciating each word. "Bennett's Hardware, of course. Earlier today, I saw you. You were right at the door and suddenly turned around and left."

I paused waiting for her to explain, but she said nothing. "Why didn't you stop in to say hello or at least tell me why you couldn't stay. You've never done that before."

She gave a short, sort of strangled, chuckle. "Now I remember. I'm sorry, dear. I'm sure, from your viewpoint, it seemed out of character. But there has been so much on my mind, I wasn't thinking. I'll explain."

Taking a breath, she launched into a plausible explanation. "I was all set to stop in for a chat, but I noticed you were busy with a customer. Dear, I realized I interrupt you too often. I get tangled up in my own motives, and I'm not sensitive to the fact you might be busy."

This was true. There were many times she'd done that. "Uh huh."

"I'm sorry, dear. I probably looked like a crazy woman. On top of not wanting to interrupt you, it occurred to me that I was expected at a meeting. And I was going to be very late. You know I pride myself at being punctual, so I had to run. I couldn't believe I'd forgotten. My memory is not what it used to be. I suppose it's the aging process."

"Completely understandable." Yep. She'd noticed it, too.

"Where was your meeting?"

"Oh, um, the library. I'd arranged to meet Lois to discuss plans for the charity book sale. There I was, standing at Bennett's, completely on the wrong side of town, at the very time I should have been arriving at the library. I knew Lois would be getting off work so I had to hurry. I ran all the way."

"You ran all the way to the library?"

"Well, of course I didn't actually run. I walked as fast as I could."

"Did you catch her?"

"What?"

"Did you get to the library in time to see Lois, before she left?"

"Oh, no. I was too late." She laughed. "I'll see her tomorrow. I have to ring off, now. They're offering some training for the meal delivery team at the community center."

I put my phone away, wondering if I was being overly suspicious. Or was my mother losing her mind?

Chapter Four

Tea drinking has spanned multiple cultures and thousands of years. A nice cup of tea has long been a favorite remedy for the anxious heart. This from my friend Clair, who is a fountain of useful information. She advocated the herbal variety in particular. Clair had suggested I keep some in stock for emergencies and had even gifted me a few kinds. This seemed like a good time to try it out.

The tea bags were in the pantry, somewhere. I ducked inside and sorted through boxes, looking for the names Chamomile and Lemon Balm. Those were Clair's favorites for calming a stressed-out mind. I wondered which one would have the strongest effect.

While inside the walls of the pantry, I heard a cell phone jingle somewhere in the distance. It was mine and I'd left it in the living room.

Pushing out of the pantry, I hustled to catch the call before it went to voicemail. My brother's name was on the screen once I'd managed to answer it. This was a worry. He never called me. Any news from him generally came through my mother or sometimes my sister-in-law, Julie.

"Hi, Chad. What's up?"

"There's something I've wanted to talk to you about. It's about Mom."

"Oh, gosh. What's happened? I just talked to her. Has she had an accident?" I hushed my voice. "It isn't about her mind, is it?"

"What? No. She's fine. And why would you ask about her mind? Do you think she's having mental problems?"

"No, no. Forget that. What did you want to talk about? What about Mom?"

"You're gonna think I'm crazy."

"That's nothing new, Little Brother, but I'm still willing to listen."

"Very funny." He paused and took a breath. "I'm going to say something, and I want you to promise not to tell her I brought it up."

"Um. Okay. I guess I can promise that. Now tell me what's on your mind."

"Okay, here it is." He paused again, sending several worst-case scenarios flashing through my thoughts. "You know Mom spends a lot of time at the church. She works with the pastor and the rest of the staff a lot."

"Uh-huh. That's not surprising since she joins every ministry team and volunteers for anything she can find."

His voice hushed. "Do you think there's anything weird going on between Mom and Pastor Prescott?"

"Weird? I haven't noticed anything out of the ordinary. That part of her life has seemed the same as it's always been. Tell me why you're asking."

"Well, I didn't think anything about it until Julie said something." Chad paused, "I mentioned seeing Mom's car at the church in the evening. It's been a couple times a week, pretty regularly. And Julie said it didn't look good. It would cause people to talk."

"Our mother is always in some kind of church meeting. Why is it different, now?"

"It's because of the time. As you know, I get off work late. Usually at 7:30 or after, and I drive past the church on the way home. Her car has been parked in the lot at least twice a week. Before you say anything, the only cars in the lot have been her little green VW and the pastor's gray Chevy. Don't you think eight at night seems kind of late to discuss church business? I mean for someone her age. And twice a week? What's up with that?"

"Are you insinuating what I think you are?"

He breathed out a deep breath. "Yeah. I'm thinking an affair."

"Ah, no. That's crazy. I'm sure it's some kind of ministry meeting and there are more people than just the two of them."

He was quiet.

"Are you sure it's even Mom's car?"

"Who else in this town drives a pea green VW?"

"Yeah. I know it's hard to miss." She had gotten a great buy because the car had sat on the lot for so long. George Trainer had taken it in as a trade-in only to discover nobody else wanted it. My mother always felt sorry for unwanted things.

I took time to mull over my brother's thoughts. "I suppose eight p.m. is kind of late for our mother. She's always in bed by nine. It would have to be a serious matter to keep her out so late."

"That's what I was thinking. Think about it, she and the pastor were in the building, alone."

"Chad, no! There's absolutely zero possibility of

anything going on between Mom and the pastor. Think about who we're talking about. He's a man of the cloth. And our mother is the most conservative widow in town. They are the holiest people I know."

"I guess you're right. She won't even watch a television program if it hints of inappropriate relationships."

She had made it difficult for us to watch any popular movies in our teen years.

"Listen, Little Brother. I'm certain there's no problem. It's probably the only time the pastor has an opening in his schedule. And there would always be someone else with them, probably his wife. And let's remember their age. Both of them are grandparents."

"It does sound silly now that you mention it. But I think you should talk to her about it anyway."

"Me? How would you have me broach the subject? Shall I tell her that her son wants to know if she's having an affair with the preacher?"

"No. But you could bring it up in conversation. Not the affair. Ask her about her church activities. It has to be you. She talks to you more than she does to me. Please look into it. I think it's important."

Since when did my younger brother start worrying about our mother's social life? Still, he must consider it important to have called me.

I let out a groan and kicked the wall. "Okay. I'll question her about meetings with the pastor. She'll wonder why I need to ask because she tells me everything. She's never mentioned anything in the evening."

"Remember, don't tell her I said anything. I don't want her to think we're talking behind her back."

"We are."

"Yeah, but she doesn't have to know. Here's an idea. Maybe mention you stopped by to see her on Tuesday night and were surprised that she wasn't at home."

"So now you want me to lie to our mother. But I'm to make sure she doesn't know you had any part in it."

"Now you've got it."

Aargh. "Okay, then. I'll figure out a way to find out what's going on."

Have I mentioned that I'm a terrible liar? Especially to my mother. She can read it in my face.

I clicked off and began to fabricate a reason for my call. It needed to be on the phone so she couldn't see my lying eyes.

Where was that herbal tea? Back in the kitchen, I tossed both Chamomile and Lemon Balm into the pot. Double the calming power. After downing a cup and doing some deep breathing exercises, I made the deceitful call.

"Hey, Mom. How are you today?"

"I'm fine dear. How are you?" I detected doubt in her voice. She already knew I was planning to lie.

"Oh, fine. I was thinking about you and thought I'd call." Awkward silence. Then, trying to sound casual. "I stopped by your house last night, but you weren't home."

"You did? I'm sorry I missed you. What did you want?"

Darn. That didn't work out. I'd planned that she would offer information. "Umm. No reason, really. Well, I wanted to borrow your muffin pans." Why did I say that? This is what happened to me when I made up stuff on the fly. My mother was well aware I never baked.

I plunged ahead, digging a deeper hole. "Thought I'd

try banana nut bread muffins and then realized I don't have a muffin pan."

"Oh, I thought you had one."

"Nope. Well, I might have, at one time, but guess I threw it away. Wouldn't you know I'd get a craving for muffins."

"You are more than welcome to mine. Do you want to come pick them up? Or I can bring them to you."

"No." I needed to keep her on the phone. Not face to face. "There's no need for you to go out, and I won't use them until tomorrow night."

"Really? When I get a craving, I want it right away. I'm happy to drive over with the pans."

"Nope. I can wait."

"Okay, dear. I'll drop them off at the office tomorrow when I go out. Or I could bake you some muffins and bring them by. How would that be?"

"That would be so nice of you but I should learn to bake my own. By the way, I..."

"Speaking of baking, I have a pie in the oven and have to get it out before it burns. So, I'll see you tomorrow."

"Great. See you then."

The line went silent and I clicked off my phone. What just happened? I didn't get the information I wanted. She was so nice to me while I lied to her. Shame on me.

And now I had to make muffins. My mother would expect to see muffins.

Worse yet, I'd committed to talking to her in person where she could read my facial expressions. I would have to spend the rest of the day practicing my innocent face. And I hoped no one else would be around the office or my mother would strike up a conversation with them. I'd never get my chance to question her.

~~

So, true to her word, my mother walked into Bennett's Hardware with the muffin pans. I caught her at the door and probed her about new ministries, old ministries, board meetings, and about everything I could think of.

She probably thought I'd lost my mind, and I never got the answer I was looking for. She said she hadn't been working at the church any more often than usual. Then she began telling me about how rewarding her church work was. And since I was so interested, I would be welcome to join her. I pressed my lips together, tucked the muffin tins under my arm, and gave up the questioning.

I was never able to pin her down as to a time schedule. If she had pressed me on why I needed to know all the details of her life, I would have lost my nerve, confessed my deception, and blamed it all on my little brother.

In the end, I concluded that there was nothing for us to worry about. Either my mother was hiding something from me—not possible—or my brother was mistaken—easily possible.

That mental debate plagued me for the rest of the day.

My mother would never do anything wrong, and if she did it was her business, not mine. Wait, as her adult daughter, and someday her caretaker, it was my business.

On my walk home, I grabbed a bench at Bird Song Park and rang my friend and advisor, Clair. After I'd gone into detail about Chad's suspicions and my own, I could imagine her rolling her eyes and shaking her head. "You and your brother are paying too much attention to what your mother is doing. You know she has never committed a sin in her life and most likely has never entertained a wicked thought. And if she has, it isn't for you to judge."

I kept my mouth shut. Clair was right.

"Unless Arnie calls you from the police station to tell you he has Katherine in a cell, don't worry about it."

I laughed and said good-bye.

But as I continued my trek home, I did worry.

Chapter Five

One more pass through the lot, before I'd have to settle for parking in the back row. Who taught these people to drive? Did they think they could park any old way just because they were at church? I finally found a place third row in and gave a little prayer of thanks for my compact Honda. I wedged it between a pickup truck sitting on the line, and a Cadillac parked barely inside its space.

It would have been easier to leave my car on the street, if I'd wanted to wreck my hair walking to the church. I made a mental note to keep quiet about the weekly struggle of stowing my automobile. My mother loved to remind me of how much easier it would be to find parking spot if I arrived earlier.

I killed the engine, jumped out, and launched into a speed walk across the lot. I thought about jogging, but my new little leather pumps with the two-inch heel weren't exactly running shoes.

I reached the church building and puffed a greeting to Mr. Johnson as he tugged the heavy door open to let me in.

"Good morning, Libby. Nice to see you. Don't you look nice today." He'd welcomed me every Sunday morning for the last.... I don't know how many years. He moved a lot slower than he used to and was looking a bit frail. But I could always count on the Twin Fawn Community Church official greeter to make the hustle across the parking lot worthwhile. No matter that he complimented me in exactly the same way every week. I couldn't remember a time when he wasn't glad to see me. Or when he didn't have a full head of brilliant white hair.

Recently, I'd made a point of trying out a new compliment for him every week. "Thank you, Mr. Johnson. You look dashing. Great tie. Is it new?" Not likely. I was pretty sure it was the same one he'd worn every week for the last two years.

This brought a chuckle from the old man. "You flatter me, Libby." He turned to greet another late arrival.

Aisles were blocked as the throng of parishioners rushed to finish conversations before the beginning of the service. I would like to have been patient with the lack of flow, but I knew my mother would be waiting for me—impatiently.

Weaving my way through, I glimpsed my friend Clair and lifted a hand to wave. I'd invited her to this church a year ago when she and her husband Michael had relocated to Twin Fawn. As I swung my gaze back toward the front, I connected with the worried frown of my mother. One arm over the seat back, she scanned the room. It was the same watchful expression she wore every week, until I took my seat beside her.

As if she thought I might not arrive. For goodness sakes, I'd been next to her in the first pew every week since being released from kids' church. But there was that look. Expectant and a little irritated. I felt the familiar tension and the urge to pick up the pace. My mother waited.

"Excuse me, Mrs. Barnes. I'll just slide around you." I scooted past the big woman, spied a clear pathway and stepped into it. Unfortunately, the aisle hadn't cleared as much as I'd imagined. Before I knew it, I was tumbling into the middle of the aisle. I reached out to latch on to the nearest sleeve and found one that saved me from a serious fall. In the process, I'd bumped into poor Mrs. Lambert and sent her stumbling forward a few steps.

Mr. Lambert steadied his wife and spoke to me. "Careful Libby. No need to hurry. God will wait for you." Chuckles erupted around me. At that moment, I did not appreciate the humor.

I looked for the person whose arm I still gripped. Dark brown eyes, crinkled at the corners. Garrett Reed. "Thank you, Garrett. You saved me." Rescued for the second time that week, but I didn't have time to elaborate. Neither did I want to admit that the two occasions would be seared into my memory.

He leaned in. "Anytime. Are you okay?" Oh my. That smoldering voice lit a little fire in my stomach.

"I'm fine, thanks to you. Just clumsy this morning." Such a lame response. Why couldn't I think of something clever and flirty?

Dimples appeared on each side of his smile. He winked and, as soon as I released his arm, he drifted into the crowd.

I spun to discover what or who had caused my fall. "I'm so sorry." I said to the owner of a rather large foot sticking out of place in the middle of the aisle. A black work boot, none too clean. Remembering where I was, just in time, I pushed down the word my mother would frown upon. I followed the boot up the dusty dark pants, to a muscled clean-shaven face, and mass of shaggy graying hair.

The man stared at me, and I rushed to apologize a second time, because my mother taught me right. "Please excuse me. I'm so sorry. I should be watching where I'm headed." I felt very righteous for that apology because I knew he was at fault. The man's foot shouldn't have been sticking out in the middle of the aisle.

He looked familiar, and I began to sort through mental images to come up with a name.

"No problem, miss. No harm done." The voice vibrated deep and rough. This man might have been a lifelong smoker. His eyes were penetrating, unsettling, but there seemed to be a smile mixed into the gaze.

Without another word the man turned to take a seat in the third to the last row. I continued the trek to my place beside Mother, who still watched for me. On the way, it dawned that the work boot I'd tripped over belonged to Big Foot of the hardware store. So sorry for calling you Big Foot, sir. Now I felt really guilty for my unkind wit. After all, the man was in church. But I couldn't get the name out of my mind, now.

My rushed and eventful Sunday morning trip left me flustered, and I'd built up some defensiveness by the time I reached my mother. Words flew out of my mouth before I thought. "I'm not late. The music hasn't even started." This was never the best way to start out a Sunday morning. But regret doesn't call the words back.

My mother replied in her usual quiet calm voice. "I know, dear. It's just that I've been here for a while. I like to watch for you."

"You were early." I couldn't help it. Still feeling

grumpy.

"Yes. I like to have time to prepare for worship. You should try it. I bet you'd be more at peace and get more enjoyment from the sermon." A sweet smile sneaked across her face before she glanced over her shoulder again.

I thought I'd try to make up for being snippy. "You're always calm. I bet you've always been at peace. Is it because of church attendance? Have you always attended? Did Grandma and Grandpa take you every week, like you did Chad and me?"

At first it appeared she wasn't listening to me, but I heard her mutter. "Not all the time." She glanced at me. "By the way, how were the muffins?"

"Muffins? Oh. Haven't made any yet. The craving went away." Yikes. I'd all but forgotten that deceit.

She raised her eyebrows but gazed back into the crowd.

When she swung her attention back to me, her forehead was creased. "Who was that man?"

"What man?" My brain had been doing a happy dance that she didn't pursue the muffin tin gambit.

"The big man I saw you speaking to at the back."

"Oh, I don't know. Just someone I tripped over. All I know is he has big feet. I think he must be new in town." I thought to add some information. My mother liked information. "He came into Bennett's earlier this week."

She squinted at me. "He was at the hardware store. I wonder what he's doing here. Do you think he might be following you?"

I almost laughed, but Mom was serious. "There's no way he would know where I went to church. This is a small town with one hardware store and not many churches. We bump into everyone at one time or another. Sometimes you worry about the silliest things."

More lines formed across her forehead as she stretched to peer through the crowd behind us. "I have a bad feeling about him. Call it an intuition."

This time I did laugh. "Relax. I doubt very much that the man is following me. It's a coincidence. That's all."

She took a breath and smiled. "Yes. I suppose you're right."

After a moment, her focus turned to my health. "Did you say you tripped? Are you hurt? Are your ankles okay?" She had leaned over and seemed to be critiquing my shoes. My mother never wore high heels.

"I'm fine. Garrett caught me." I imagined him reaching out with both hands and taking me into his arms. "Well, he didn't catch me so much as I latched on to his arm to keep from falling." With his dark eyes and smooth voice resonating in my memory, I couldn't help but smile.

My mother has always been adept at reading my mind. "You can do much better than Garrett Reed. He's dated about every girl in town. Look for someone who is stable."

"How do you know how many girlfriends he's had?"

"Liberty, this is a small town. You know there are no secrets in Twin Fawn."

I waved the discussion away. "Anyway, I didn't say I was interested in him. Only that he kept me from making a fool of myself in the middle of the aisle."

"Hmm." She returned her attention to the stage as the music began.

Halfway through the hymn, I caught her sneaking a

peak into the crowd. It wasn't like my mother to allow her mind to wander. I leaned toward her and whispered. "Who are you looking for?"

She used her evasive motherly smile. "No one."

Unlike my mother, my attention often wandered in church. I sat considering whether I should be concerned about her. "Are you feeling alright? You seem a little pale." Had she been taking care of herself? She'd been alone for almost a year since my father's fatal heart attack, and I'd read about widows sometimes neglecting themselves.

"I'm fine, dear." She effectively cut off conversation by directing her eyes to the front. Church had begun.

My mind still drifting, I leaned toward her and whispered. "Were you looking for my little brother? You know Chad and Julie never get here until right before the message. They can't seem to get the boys dressed on Sunday morning." I harbored some jealousy that my brother had escaped the mandatory front row seating arrangement once he got married. He and Julie opted for the safety of the mid-section and mother didn't object. It made her nervous when one of them would have to get up to check on her grandsons in the toddler room.

She whispered in return, "I know they'll be here. Now, shush."

I shushed.

We were in the middle of *Be Thou My Vision* when I swiveled to glance at the crowd behind us. A mass of familiar faces. I'd met almost everyone. My mother made it a point to welcome newcomers, and usually dragged me along, hoping I'd develop the talent. She would probably even seek out the man with the poorly placed boot, bad feeling or not.

Before I finished my scan of the crowd, I caught site of Garrett, sitting next to Lovey Henderson. She'd been homecoming queen in high school. Married the quarter back and was now divorced. She proudly maintained her title as most popular girl in town and had inherited a good job managing her parent's clothing store. She and Garrett were talking during the singing. I guess that was a perk of not sitting in the front row next to one's mother.

It had always been an unquestioned rule that we sat there, in that very visible place. My parents gave me the impression that we received some sort of special blessing per the seating arrangement. As a child, I imagined we were closer to God. Later, I realized it was closer to Pastor Prescott.

The pastor droned on. My mind wandered, intermittently. I should have been listening and taking notes. My mother would be so proud if we could discuss the sermon over lunch.

I'd grown up in that little church. The same seat, although they'd updated from pews to chairs a few years back. Fourth seat to the right of the center aisle. I pictured my father and little brother on my left. My mother on the right.

Every week of my life, except the one time of rebellion as a teen. I'd feigned illness to stay at home. Mother hovered over me, took my temperature, set a cup of tea beside me. I thought I might have overdone it. That she might skip the service to care for me, but at the last minute, she pulled away promising to return as soon as possible. As the family drove out of the driveway I popped from my bed and flipped on the television.

I leafed through magazines and found some cookies in the kitchen, but got myself tucked back into bed by the time my brother tramped up the stairs to change his clothes.

Mother climbed the stairs next, hurrying to check on me. "I prayed for you. That you would feel better and that you wouldn't be afraid being alone."

There it was, the guilt. "It worked, Mom. I feel much better now. I think I'll have a little lunch." In truth, that's when I began to feel sick. I'd lied to my kind, loving mother. And she'd pulled God into it. I would go to hell for sure. That was my first and last attempt at being a wayward child. I'm a rule follower, like my mother.

Dad, a postman, never missed a delivery despite rain or snow or sleet until the fatal heart attack released him from his earthly duties. Mom, part-time librarian, kept a quiet library and managed to earn the love and respect of everyone in town.

Maybe it was true. Blessings came with the front-row seat.

Sermon over, we rose and made our way to the aisle. I took my time, knowing I'd wait while my mother exchanged a few words with those sitting around us. I smiled and nodded but rarely joined the conversation. After a greeting, I quit listening and watched the congregation file out.

I saw no sign of the big-footed man. Should I worry that I'd run into the ominous stranger twice within a few days? Or should I be more concerned about Mother's unusually accurate intuition?

Chapter Six

Hallelujah. My mother had returned to my side. "Have you exhausted all topics of conversation, so soon?"

She grinned. "There wasn't much to talk about today. Besides I knew you were waiting to go to lunch."

We filed out of the church and discussed where we would meet, deciding on Lucy's Café, a favorite of the after-church crowd. Mother waved as she climbed into her car. "I'll call your brother and ask if he and the family would like to meet us."

~~

My stomach rumbled as I spoke to the hostess to request a table for six. I returned to give Mother the bad news of a thirty-minute wait and found her staring into the distance—at nothing, or more accurately, a blank wall.

I sat beside her. "It will be about half an hour before we get a table." I expected a complaint about that, or at least a groan but received no response. She seemed to be lost in never-never land. I raised my voice a notch. "Mother."

She snapped to attention and focused on me. "I'm sorry, dear. I guess I was daydreaming. What did you say?"

"I said there's a thirty-minute wait."

She smiled. "Okay."

"Really? Are you satisfied with waiting that long? We could try somewhere else."

"It will be fine. I like Lucy's."

I leaned back on the bench. "I'm surprised. I thought you would have plans for this afternoon. Something at the church?"

She sat fidgeting with her purse. "Those duties will wait. And, this way, we will have more time to talk."

"Is there anything in particular that you want to talk about?"

"No. Just things in general, dear."

I stood to watch for my brother and his family. "I haven't seen Chad and Julie. What's taking them so long?"

My mother stared at me for a moment. It seemed I'd brought her back from a daydream again. "Oh, they're not coming. When I called to let them know we'd be here, Chad said they couldn't meet us today."

That would have been nice to know. "Oh, then we only need a table for two. I'll inform the hostess." I did an about face and returned to the hostess station. After amending the request for table size, I made my way back to my mother. "Ten minutes."

She leaned toward me. "I'm sorry. I should have told you they cancelled, but it slipped my mind."

A sweet smile crossed her face. The grandmotherly smile that always showed up when she thought of my nephews. "Lunch won't be the same without those boys. They're so entertaining. Don't you think so?"

I tried to resist the eye roll. Lord, help me, I loved my

nephews, but at three and four years of age, they didn't have the capacity to sit still for more than two minutes. I wouldn't miss the squirming and the teasing pokes at one another.

Mom stared into the distance. "I wonder if the boys are old enough to help in the soup kitchen? I'd like to start teaching them about service."

I blinked at her, the image of a food fight flashing through my mind. Before I could dash my mother's dream, the hostess called my name and led the way to a table.

After a few minutes of browsing the menu, my mother laid hers on the table. "I was thinking about that man you were talking to."

I glanced back to the hostess station. "What man? I don't remember talking to anyone except the waitress."

She leaned forward and looked into my eyes. "Not here, dear. The man you were talking to at the church before the service."

I squinted at her.

She sighed. "It was when you were on your way in. Don't you remember? Honestly, Liberty. I worry about your short-term memory."

"My memory is fine. Are you referring to the guy who tripped me? He wasn't all that memorable. And we weren't talking. I told you, his foot was in the aisle."

"What was his name?"

"I didn't get it. There wasn't time for formal introductions. Church was about to begin. I apologized and went on my way. Why?"

She narrowed her gaze and clucked her tongue. "No reason. There was something about him. It just didn't feel right. So, don't let him approach you again."

I began to worry about my mother's fixations. "For goodness sakes, I wouldn't say he approached me. We just got our feet tangled up. It isn't something that is likely to happen again." I went back to scanning the menu, weighing the merits of a tuna salad versus turkey club sandwich, but continued to sense her gaze resting on me. Perhaps a little reassurance? "I doubt I'll ever see him again."

With a shake of her head, she picked up her menu. "I didn't like the looks of him."

I put my menu on the table. "I've never known you to judge a person on his appearance. You're the one who is always telling me God looks on the heart, not the outside." I smiled, proud of myself for remembering something biblical.

Mother straightened. "It really isn't about his looks, just something about him. A warning bell that I can't explain. We get those feelings, you know. They're for our protection. So, watch out for yourself. You might see him again. It's a small town. If that happens, stay away. Give him a wide berth."

"Sure. If that's what you want. But I've never known you to be so suspicious. When did you start getting psychic feelings?"

My mother glanced at me and shrugged, then went back to studying her menu. The truth was I hoped I'd never run into him. He gave me the creeps. But my mother had always been much more accepting. I would call her innocent, while I entertained a more worldly view of society.

The waitress took our orders, and we filled the time, or my mother did, with a discussion of the pastor's sermon.

When we received our sandwiches, I concentrated on devouring mine. She had taken only one or two bites when she put hers down.

"Have you had any more unexpected visitors?"

I stopped mid-bite. "What?" Where did that come from?

"Have any of the neighbors wandered in again? Remember? The other day you thought someone had come into the house."

"Oh. I'd forgotten." I was having a hard time keeping up with Mom's train of thought. "No one has wandered in. I'm sure it was a one-time thing." I returned to my lunch.

I'd forgotten about the incident, but my mother hadn't. The woman never forgot a need. In this instance there might be someone she could help, and she wouldn't let a good cause pass her by.

She took a bite of her sandwich but seemed too concerned with a wandering neighbor to enjoy it. "I called everyone on the block. All of them, even the young people. Everyone seems to be fine. No reports of memory lapses. I suppose it was someone with their thoughts on other things, like you said." She sat quietly for a moment. "Of course, if a person was experiencing a memory issue, they might not even realize it."

My mother could sometimes become obsessed. I searched for normal conversation, where I wouldn't have to worry about her mental health. "What do you have planned for the rest of the afternoon?"

She smiled. "As soon as we're done here, I'll go back to the church and organize the food pantry."

"Today? Can't it wait? I thought there was something in the Bible about Sunday being a day of rest." Another

Bible reference. I was on a roll.

"That's true, but I just haven't had time to get it done. Considering what God has done for me, I owe the Lord all of my time."

How could I argue with her?

Between bites, I made another attempt to divert her attention. "Mrs. Porter has a new hairstyle. She's cut it shorter. Looks nice on her, doesn't it?"

Mission accomplished. She fell into step, but quickly settled her attention on me. "Liberty, look over there. It's Lloyd Hamilton. Such a nice young man. I think he's teaching history at the high school this year. He's alone. Let's ask him to join us."

I'd taken a sip of water and nearly choked, spitting it halfway across the table. "No Mom. We're finished." I blotted the water with my napkin.

"We could have desert while he has lunch."

"I don't want desert, and I thought you just told me you had work to do." I was frantic. Sure didn't want to spend an hour making conversation with one of the most boring men in Twin Fawn. He talked history. Nothing else, not even the interesting parts of history, as if there were any.

She pushed ahead. "But..."

"Oh, too bad." I said a little prayer of thanks when Lloyd waved to someone on the other side of the restaurant. "He's meeting someone."

Probably every mother in town considered Lloyd Hamilton the perfect catch. Those of us who were not over fifty considered him excessively tall, unseasonably pale, and just plain bland.

"Oh, that's a shame. He's so interesting. It would have been nice to have his company at lunch. Maybe some other time."

I took a big swig of water to keep from screaming. Then I thought it would be better to be clear, rather than revisit the subject in the coming weeks. "No. Please don't ever invite him to join us. I'm sure he's a very nice man, but he is not for me. I've never, ever seen him laugh. He doesn't even smile."

"That just means he's serious minded. You have to think about the future, Liberty. A girl needs a man who is stable, who won't fly off on a tangent, and who will be able to support a family.

"Why are we talking about marriage all of a sudden? I'm only thirty-five. Plenty of time."

My mother picked up her napkin and tucked it under her plate. "No hurry dear. Just making conversation."

Maybe I would turn the tables. "Since we're talking about men, what do you think of Mr. Bennett?"

"Stanley? What do you mean? He's a nice man and seems to be a good employer. Don't you like him?"

"Sure, I like him. I brought him up because I think if you encouraged him, he would ask you out. You've been alone since Dad died and Mr. Bennett is so nice. The two of you would make a cute couple."

"What? Liberty Breeze, I'm much too busy—and too old—to date."

"You aren't too old for companionship."

"Enough, Liberty. I will not start dating at this point in my life. I don't want to hear anything more about it."

Thankfully, the waitress showed up with our bill. I supplied my credit card.

While we waited for her return, my mother became distracted again. "Liberty, since you don't seem to be interested in Lloyd, maybe Maximus Bailey is more your style."

I stared at her and forgot to breathe. I squeaked, "Maximus?"

"Yes." She nodded toward the door, where the man, who no one ever called Max, was standing at the cash register. "He's a successful farmer. I bet he's smart, because it isn't easy to make a small farm profitable around here."

The man cast a wide shadow at the front of the restaurant. Maximus was a tall, bulky presence.

"I'm not interested in him." Redirecting her again. "Think about it, Mom, when you were young did you like the guys your parents wanted you to date?"

I knew she had heard me but she continued as if she hadn't. "You like animals. And your flower garden was beautiful this year. I bet you have a lot in common. Maybe you should show him some interest."

Staring at the woman, unable to answer. I tried to force a smile but my face was frozen.

It took a minute before she gradually sensed my mood. "You don't have to look so horrified. Since your father passed, it's my responsibility to be concerned with your welfare and your protection. We were secure when he was here. He kept us safe."

"I'm fine, Mom. I don't need anyone to protect me. We're in Twin Fawn, Indiana, for goodness sakes. What self-respecting criminal would be caught dead in a town named Twin Fawn?"

She shrugged and took a sip of water. "That's a valid point."

Why was my mother so concerned with my safety? Was it paranoia or the beginning of dementia?

A feeling of dread was seeping into my heart. Yes,

I'd always felt safe when my father was alive, but Twin Fawn hadn't changed. Why shouldn't I feel secure now?

Chapter Seven

"If you want my opinion, the problem is that both you and your mother live alone. Too much time to think," Headlights lit Clair's face for a moment and then left it in shadows as cars passed. We'd spent the evening at Morelli's Irish Pub, which happened to be the best place in Twin Fawn for Italian cuisine, and Irish whiskey if you happened to be into that sort of thing. We were driving back to my place to catch a movie. Clair always insisted on driving. Her BMW being more comfortable than my Honda.

She glanced at me and continued her analysis of life. "Katherine grew up depending on her father and then her husband for support. That's what women did. Believe me, it's not a bad thing. I love that I have Michael to share the expenses and chores around the house. Even though we know you are perfectly capable of taking care of yourself, understand that your mom is bound to worry. She feels like she has sole responsibility."

Clair reached over and tapped my arm. "I know. Why don't we fix her up with Stanley? They'd make such a cute couple. Both of them sweet and peaceful. Wouldn't it be nice for them to have companionship in their later years?"

"Already thought of that and Mom wouldn't even discuss it." I leaned my head on the seat back. "Sorry I've been complaining all night. You were nice enough to go out with me, and you've had to listen to me groan."

"Not to worry. That's what friends are for." Clair waved a hand in my direction. "When did Katherine start acting like this? You've never said anything before."

"That's the strange thing. It was recently. I can't say exactly when, but it's become worse in the last couple of weeks." I sat for a few minutes, then gasped. "Do you think she's had a stroke?"

Clair laughed. "Now you've gone off the deep end. She hasn't had a stroke. She's being a typical mother. It's natural. You'll always be her little girl, no matter how old you are. Get used to it" My friend paused to negotiate a turn. "You might remind her I didn't meet Michael until I was older than you are."

Clair slowed and veered into my driveway. "I was perfectly happy with my life and my career. Then he showed up and I was even happier. You have plenty of time."

We came to a stop. I pushed the car door open and slid out. "No more talk about my troubles. This is a beautiful night. Listen to the crickets."

"It's a perfect autumn evening."

I leaned against the hood of the BMW. "What's the movie you wanted to see?"

"*Fifteen Ghosts of Strawberry Lane*, or something like that. But we have time. I love listening to the night sounds."

We stood in the light of the BMW's delayed headlights, listening to the crickets and recounting the events of the evening.

Clair gave me a sly smile. "You know, there was that guy at the next table tonight. I think he liked you. You could have encouraged him."

"Oh please. We've already discussed that part of my life. My mother spends enough time trying to fix me up."

"Okay, Lib. Let's get inside. I don't want to miss the beginning of the movie." Clair took a step toward the house and that was the last I saw of her because everything became very dark.

"Eek! Who turned out the lights?" I held on to the BMW's hood, hoping my eyes would adjust to the lack of light.

"Oops. I didn't think we'd stood here that long." I heard my friend's voice but could barely discern the shadowy area where she stood. Or I thought she stood.

"Keep talking because I can't see a thing. It's eerie out here." The streetlights provided illumination reaching only a fraction of the way across the lawn, leaving my house shrouded in darkness.

I heard Clair giggle. "Isn't this the perfect night for a horror flick? There's no moon, not even a star." Her voice dropped to a whisper. "I wonder what's out there in the dark."

"Stop. Don't get me started imagining things."

"I can flip the headlights on again."

"No. Don't bother. I know the way."

I took a guess as to where Clair stood and reached out to grasp her arm. When I made contact, I latched on and awkwardly stepped up beside her. "Okay, I'll guide us to the house. Be careful and don't trip. Remember my sidewalk is uneven." We linked arms and giggled as we slowly picked our way toward the house.

"Girl, why didn't you leave the porchlight on?

There's not even a lamp on in the window. For all I know, we could be heading in the wrong direction."

"I didn't think about it. When am I ever out late enough to need to leave a light on? Stay with me. I'm steering you toward the house. It isn't far to the steps."

Clair gasped and stopped abruptly. "What's that noise. It sounds like someone sneaking up on us. I strained my ears and held my breath for a moment. Letting out the breath, I sighed. "It's the bushes. The wind is blowing them against the house."

"Geesh. It had me scared to death." Clair's giggle had turned strained. "Let's go." We steadied each other for the rest of our blind trek to safety. The breeze rustled through the bushes again, and I felt my friend tremble. Or it might have been me.

"Next time, let's take more care in choosing topics of discussion while we're out. I'm thinking the scariest flicks of all time, and after that the dangers you face while living alone, weren't the best."

We shuffled up the walk until my toes finally touched the bottom step. I reached for the railing and guided us to the porch. Clair clung to my jacket until I managed to fit the key into the lock. With my first push the door creaked with an unearthly squeal.

"Yikes." Clair stomped her foot. "Don't you have an oil can? You work at a hardware store, for goodness sakes."

She lowered her voice. "Wait. Did you set this up to scare me? If you did, it's working."

"Are you kidding? That door's been squeaking since I moved in. Haven't you noticed it before?"

"No. It must be louder in the dark."

There was another loud squawk as I shoved it wide

so we could both fit through. "You're right, it's worse in the dark. I'll get some oil and fix it tomorrow."

We stood in the foyer while I fumbled to find the light switch. The hall light sparked to life, but just as quickly fizzled and went out.

We froze, speechless, until Clair laughed. "This is too much." She began a passable Vincent Price impression. "Who knows what's on the other side of this door. Are you sure you want to enter? It's the haunted house on Strawberry Lane. Run for your life while you still can."

"Stop or I will run for my life." I laughed, but noticed I was trembling as well. "Hold on." I shuffled further into the house and slapped my hand across the living room wall until I came into contact with the light switch. The lamps sprang to life and, thankfully, stayed that way.

After tossing my jacket and bag on the couch I trotted to the kitchen. "I'll get the popcorn and something to drink while you find the channel. The movie's about to start."

I pulled a couple colas from the refrigerator and set them on the counter while I found the bag of White Cheddar Popcorn in the pantry.

I'd filled glasses with ice when a thump rattled the wall and prompted me to check on my friend. I yelled. "What did you run into?" No answer. Had she dropped something? Or fallen?

I made quick work of pouring cola into glasses while scanning my memory to think of anything Clair might have tripped over.

Clair was still on her feet when I carried the refreshments to the living room. I positioned them on the coffee table, while taking a stealthy glance around.

Nothing seemed to be out of place. "Okay. What happened?"

"Huh?" Clair reached into the bag and brought out a fistful of popcorn.

"I heard you crash into something and wondered if I should come in here to help. I don't see anything broken." I continued the scan, wondering if a lamp had fallen.

"It wasn't me. It was you." She gave me a crooked smile. "You're still trying to scare me. I heard you drop something in the kitchen." Her voice dropped to a whisper. "Did you break something of your mothers? I'm not taking the blame for it."

I leveled my gaze on Clair. "I'm serious. I heard a noise. The wall even vibrated. What was it?"

Clair stared at me for a moment. "There was a crash, but it wasn't in here. I honestly thought it was you." She twisted to peer into the hallway leading to the bathroom. "If you didn't do it, and I didn't, who was it?"

I blew out a breath. "It must have been outside. It's windy, and the neighbors have a bunch of plastic chairs on their deck. They're always blowing around in a storm." I glanced toward the window and stepped over to close the curtains. "But as dark as it is, I'm not venturing out to check."

Clair shrugged. "As long as neither of us broke anything of your mom's we're safe. Sit down. The movie's about to begin." She pulled the popcorn close and dug in for another handful.

I sat in the recliner and pulled my feet up, wrapping my arms around my knees as the movie got into full swing with screams, groans, and thunderclaps.

Halfway through the thriller, Clair jumped up. "Keep

track of the action and fill me in when I get back from the Ladies' room. I can't wait any longer." She trotted down the hallway.

I was engrossed in the movie when, a few minutes later, Clair bounced onto the couch, "What did I miss?"

"Nothing much. Nobody got killed. One new ghost showed up in the background, but nobody noticed it."

Clair hissed. "Oooh! What did it look like?"

"A woman, I think. Long robe and scraggly hair. Only visible for a minute."

"Okay." She picked up a pillow and clutched it to her chest. "By the way. I closed the window you left open in the bathroom. It's getting cold out."

I kept my eyes on the screen. Attention glued to the action. "Thanks. I'd forgotten."

After we'd screamed and gritted our teeth through the entire movie, we breathed a sigh of relief at the not particularly satisfying finale. I clicked off the television. Clair picked up the glasses while I retrieved the empty popcorn bag as well as a few kernels that had landed on the floor. We headed for the kitchen.

Clair dumped the leftover cola into the sink and turned on the water. "It's a good thing I found the open window. There's a freeze warning tonight."

She dried her hands on a paper towel. "I'm surprised you even opened one. You're the one who is always cold."

I glanced up from tying the trash bag. "Thanks for getting it. I've had a lot on my mind lately. Just forgot to close it."

I turned on the porch light and Clair trotted to her car. She stuck her arm out the window and waved goodbye as she pulled from the drive.

Before setting the bolt lock, I took a quick look outside. Sometimes I wished there was a man around. To check the windows and doors, if nothing else.

I took a turn through the house, double checking to be sure all windows were shut and locked. I was glad Clair had found the one that had been left open. Had I opened it when I cleaned the bathroom? But the longer I mulled it over, the more convinced I became that I had *not* left that window open.

Chapter Eight

Three quick raps on the door and, "Hello. It's me." had always been my three-second warning before Clair marched into my living room. This time, however, there were three raps and a thump.

Realizing someone stood stranded on the porch, I hustled to the entryway to release the bolt lock. On opening the door, I found my friend massaging her forehead.

Clair scowled at me. "When did you start using the lock? I'm lucky I didn't break my nose."

I winced. "Ouch. Sorry, I decided to be more careful about safety and lock the door while I worked in the back bedroom. You know I've been jumpy since that morning someone walked in unannounced. It's still up in the air whether it might have been my mother, but it could easily have been some stranger off the street."

I eyed the red bump forming on Clair's forehead and waved her in. "Whoever it was, I'm determined to be more cautious. Um, should I get you an icepack?"

"No, I'm sure I'll be fine. Anyway, I had some time off and thought I'd stop in for a visit."

"I'm glad you did. I could use your help with something."

I led the way to my bedroom and pointed to a length of twine hanging from a hinged trap door inconveniently located in the ceiling of the walk-in closet.

"I've been trying my best to pull that door down so I can get into the attic. It's stuck. Who knows how long it's been since it was used? I've practically hung on that rope, but it won't budge."

Clair examined the trap door designed to swing down from the ceiling, allowing a ladder to extend out into the bedroom. At about six feet deep and just over four feet wide, the closet afforded space for most of my attire. One wall sported a pole for hanging garments. The other wall contained several shelves loaded with shoes, sweaters and other folded clothing.

"There isn't much room to work, with all your clothes packed in there. But if we pull on it together, it should come down."

Clair stepped into the closet behind me. "Grab the rope. I'm taller so I'll hold on above your hands."

I did as she suggested. She latched on and we both gave a tug. The door released easier than expected and, as it swung down, we were knocked off our feet. I fell into a stack of sweaters. Clair dislodged hangers containing my church clothes.

I fought to untangle myself and swiped a cardigan sleeve from my face. "Well, that worked."

After we regained our footing, I helped Clair re-hang the dresses. That done, we slithered around to the front of the now lowered trap door and unfolded the steps.

Clair edged close to gaze up into the black opening in the ceiling. "So, what's up there?"

"Not a thing. This is a stairway to the forever empty room. We were never allowed to put stuff up there. My mother had a rule that we store nothing. If we didn't use it regularly, we gave it away to someone in need. My brother and I thought about sneaking up here, but didn't dare, because this was my parents' room."

"I never heard of an empty attic. Mine is already full, and we've only been in the house a year. Were your grandparents strict in that way?"

"I have no idea. I always assumed they had the same rules, but I was never at their home, so can't confirm it."

"Huh. I guess it's a good way to live. Maybe I should get up in my attic and clear out a few things." My friend shifted her gaze to me. "If you don't use the attic, why did we pull the steps down?"

I pointed to two boxes sitting on my bed. "Those are full of stuff I don't use anymore and I'm putting them in the attic."

Clair leveled her eyes at me. "So, you're about to strike out on your own and break your mother's rule."

"I admit it looks that way, but in truth, I have my mother's blessing. The church's Spring rummage sale is in April, so Mom wants me to donate all my cast-offs. I don't want them sitting around the house, so it's up into the attic they go. My mother intends to have the biggest sale the church has ever seen."

"That makes sense."

"There's another reason I'm glad you stopped by. I wasn't sure how I'd get these boxes into the attic. I'll go up the ladder a few steps. You hand me the boxes from the bottom."

I started up the stairs and Clair lifted the first package. While balanced near the top I wondered at the wisdom of popping my head up through the dark hole.

A hanging light fixture was visible, so I went up

another step and reached for the pull chain. "Shoot, there's no bulb."

Still holding her burden, Clair called, "Do you want me to find a light bulb?"

"That isn't necessary. I can position both boxes near the opening."

After I stepped down again and steadied myself, I leaned down into the light. Clair shoved the box up to me. "I've got it. Thanks."

I shifted the box above my head and shoved it through the opening.

Encouraged by success, we attacked the second box and managed to get it into storage next to the first.

"While I'm here, I want to check out the attic. I pulled myself through the opening and got on my hands and knees. After sliding the boxes further to the side, I sat to contemplate this unknown space in my house. Nothing much to see in the dark, but intriguing just the same.

Scooting back to the opening I shouted to Clair. "Would you get the flashlight from the kitchen and hand it up to me? It's in the drawer on the left side of the sink. While I'm up here, I might as well take a look around. You know, check for any potential problems. Squirrels or chipmunks, or whatever."

Clair was gone for a moment and returned with the flashlight. "Do you think you have critters up there?"

I took the light and chuckled. "Gosh, I hope not. It just seems that since I'm a homeowner now, I should be watching for anything that might be a hazard. Any ideas of what I should be on the alert for?"

She planted her fists on her hips, face upturned. "I've been a realtor for years, but I couldn't tell you. I guess if you see daylight coming through the roof, you'll know there's a problem. But you won't need the flashlight for that."

"Yikes. I don't want to even think of it." There seemed to be no holes with daylight shining through, so I flipped on the flashlight and swung it around the room. I found no trace of unwanted animals but the beam did reveal something unexpected."

I called down to Clair. "I feel like I've found buried treasure. There is something stored in here after all. It must be something my folks forgot about."

Clair stood at the bottom of the steps. "What did you find? Is it a bag of money?"

"That's doubtful. I'm sure if either of my parents ever had any extra cash, they would have given it away."

I focused the light to the back of the attic. Tucked into the dark corner lay a cardboard box, apparently old, a little beat up, covered with dust and a cobweb. My first thought was to grab the garbage can and dispose of it. But if it was of any value, my mother would want it for the rummage sale. I entertained a little interest in what it might contain, but my friend couldn't suppress her curiosity.

Clair bounced on the bottom step of the ladder. "What is it? Bring it down."

"It's probably nothing. Something we'll end up putting in the sale. I might leave it here until I come back up in the Spring."

Clair jumped to the floor. "You can't just leave it. Don't you want to know what it contains?

"Where's your love for mystery? I wonder how long it's been there. I bet it's a treasure, or a map to a buried treasure. Maybe you'll find the deed to one of those mansions on the west side of town."

I glanced down at my friend. "You have a strange imagination."

I scooted on hands and knees to the corner. One dirty box, sealed with crackly old tape. "Okay. We'll open it and then, if it's worth anything, I'll repack it in a clean box." I shifted position and began shoving it to the ladder, coughing occasionally from the cloud of dust it released.

"Ugh. I can't breathe for this stuff. This box is filthy. It's going straight to the trash bin."

"You can't do that without knowing what's inside. Maybe it's a family heirloom." Clair's enthusiasm grew while any interest I'd had suffocated in the dust.

"My family doesn't have heirlooms. Remember? Everything not used always went to charity."

"Somebody stored that box for a reason. Katherine probably forgot about it, but it must have been important at one time."

I blew my bangs out of my eyes. I had to agree. "You're right. I guess I'll sort through whatever is inside. If there's anything worthwhile, we'll save it for the sale."

Clair climbed up the ladder so that her head protruded into the attic. "Hand it to me and I'll take it down."

I gave it a push. "Hold your breath. This dust is lethal."

Clair grabbed the package and transported it to the floor, where it sat shedding dirt on my bedroom carpet. She plopped down beside it and gleefully began to pull open the flaps. The old packing tape crackled and fell apart. "It's an ancient treasure. This box looks as if it has been sealed for more years than you've been around."

Clair finished tearing at the box and plunged her hand inside. "Woohoo. There is plunder in there! I knew there would be gold."

Chapter Nine

"Gold?" This got my attention, and I watched to see what she pulled from the dirty old box.

She lifted her prize above her head. "E-Town Gold!"

I stared at her. "That's not gold. It's a book."

"The high school yearbooks from Evelynton, Indiana are called E-Town Gold. There are two of them in here. I recognized the red and gold lettering right away. You know I lived in Evelynton before we moved to Twin Fawn. I used to see these yearbooks around town, even bought advertising in it one year."

"Yearbooks? They must be my mother's. She grew up there. Did you know that?"

"You said once that your grandparents used to live in Evelynton. We talked about it when I mentioned I'd lived there for about fifteen years before coming here. You'll find information about your family in these books. Your mother's picture. Maybe aunts, uncles, cousins?"

"The only relative I know who would be in these yearbooks, is my mother. She was an only child and never mentioned any cousins."

"But you told me Katherine wasn't sentimental about things. Yet, she saved her yearbooks. There must have been a few good memories."

"She sure never mentioned any. Storing this must have been a mistake. I bet she's forgotten all about it."

Clair flipped through pages of the book. "What year did she graduate?"

"I don't know. She never said."

"You never asked?"

"I guess not. You know how she loves to talk and how flighty she is. Any time I asked her to tell me about the past, she would get carried away talking about something completely unrelated."

I shook my head in an attempt to change the subject. Clair's questions had touched a nerve. Why didn't I have the answers? "Anyway, don't you think the most recent book would be her graduation year? I wouldn't mind seeing her picture."

"Don't tell me you've never seen your mother's senior picture."

"I haven't. Is that strange? We didn't have any old photographs. I never thought anything of it. At least at the time."

Clair shrugged. "I guess I don't know if it's odd or not. My parents were major collectors. Scrapbooks, mementos from the grandparents, everything. So, I thought everyone kept stuff. Anyway, here's the year nineteen seventy-two, so you'll get to see at least one photo from your mother's mysterious past."

My heart beat a little faster. Would there be a surprise in there? Would I discover anything I didn't already know?

Clair grinned as she held the book out of my reach. "Maybe you'll discover a deep dark secret."

The momentary excitement faded as I thought about

it. "Not likely. What mystery do you imagine she could hide? Her life runs on an even keel, twenty-four seven."

Clair lowered her arm and extended the book to me. "You're right. Katherine Cassell is nothing if not predictable. Don't we all wish our lives were as peaceful and organized as hers?"

Still, there might be clues to my family history in that book. I grabbed the E-Town Gold from Clair's hand. "Did they list school activities back then? I'd love to see if she took part in any clubs. But knowing my mother, she probably spent her time going to church, doing schoolwork, and reading. Not a bad thing, but not particularly exciting."

I leafed through the senior photos. "Her maiden name was Baron, so she should be toward the front."

Clair had been hovering when she suddenly placed her index finger on the second page of class photos. "There! Oh, isn't she cute? She looks very sweet, don't you think?"

I looked into eyes that hadn't changed much over the years, except for a few added creases. "She does look sweet. Look at the sweater she's wearing. Beige. Plain. Pretty much what she wears today. Fresh, clean face. Innocent." As I'd expected, my mother had always been conservative in nature.

Many of the other student photos listed high school activities, but the space beside my mother's senior portrait gave no information. She apparently hadn't been in any clubs or senior activities. I wouldn't have been surprised if teenaged Katherine Barron had dedicated her entire life to church and community projects. She was a good person even then. Her passions were probably nothing the school thought important enough to record in the yearbook.

I turned to the back of the book, where I thought it would be common for friends to sign their name and to write a personal note. One teacher, Mr. Booker, inscribed a simple, "Good luck." Nothing to give me insight into my mother's high school personality.

Clair pulled out a second E-Town Gold. "This would be the year before she graduated." My friend began to flip the pages. "Here it is. I found her junior year picture. Wow. Look at this." She pointed at the small black and white photo. "That's some heavy eyeliner. She must have liked makeup that year."

"No. That isn't her. This girl is even wearing eye shadow."

Clair leaned in. "And lipstick."

"They must have put the wrong picture next to her name." I pulled the book closer, looking past the black eyeliner and mascara. "Oh. It is her, after all." I handed the book back to Clair. "Big difference in the two years. I wonder what made the change."

Clair giggled. "I guess we know when she got religion." She glanced at me and pressed her lips together. "Sorry. That's disrespectful." She shrugged. "But it still might explain it."

"Maybe." I picked up the first yearbook for another look at her senior picture. "Maybe she just forgot to wear makeup that day."

Clair gave me a wide-eyed look. "What teenaged girl could forget to do her face on the day her picture would be taken?"

"You may be right about her becoming religious. She doesn't seem to care about makeup now." I shrugged and dug deeper into the box. More books. Agatha Christie's

Third Girl. Another Christie, *Double Sin. Red Threads – A Green Door Mystery* by Rex Stout. "Wow, I can't imagine these belonged to her. She never reads mysteries or crime novels. She tells me they're a waste of time."

My phone rang and I pulled it from my jeans pocket.

"Liberty. Hello, dear. I'm on my way to the grocery and wondered if I could pick up anything for you."

"Thanks Mom. That's nice of you but I'm still stocked up from the last time you shopped for me."

I glanced into the box of the only possessions my mother had ever saved. "By the way, I went up to the attic to store the clothes and things for the church rummage sale, like you wanted me to. While up there I found something. Did you know you have stuff stored in the attic?"

"No. It couldn't be mine. You know I don't keep anything I don't use."

"Yes, I know that very well, and I was surprised to find it. It isn't much. Just a box shoved way back in the corner. It's dark up there. That's probably why it got left."

"I can't imagine it's anything of mine. Are you sure you didn't put it up there?"

"Definitely not mine. I looked in...."

"Wait." My mother almost shrieked. She paused and resumed in a breathless rush. "I seem to remember putting something in the attic, once. Don't bother with it. Just leave it, and I'll come pick it up. There is no sense in you getting all dirty in that attic."

I laughed. "Too late. I'm covered with dust. I already pulled it out. I'll leave it in the living room, and you can pick it up whenever you want. Better yet, why don't I go through it and let you know what it contains? Then you won't have to deal with it if you don't want to."

Something warned me against admitting to having dug into my mother's things. "Do you want me to take a look? Maybe you'll want me to pitch it." I paused to breathe, experiencing some guilt for not disclosing the whole truth. "In fact, I already...."

"No. Liberty. Don't bother yourself. I'm already out and have to go past your house anyway. I'm almost there. Just stay out of it. I don't want you to get dirty. I'll be right over."

"Mom—." But she had already hung up.

I tucked the phone into my back pocket and gazed at Clair. "She's on her way. How weird. She was kind of serious about me staying out of her stuff. I don't have a clue as to why, but do you think we can put everything back in so she doesn't know we've seen it?"

Clair had been unloading it while I spoke on the phone. "Oops." She pulled out another package. "Look at this. It's jewelry, wrapped in paper bags."

"My mother doesn't even wear jewelry. Why would she have that?"

I took a deep breath. "I don't know why, but she sounded very determined that I stay out of that box. Hurry, put everything back in."

Clair shrugged, replaced the wrapped jewelry and shoved the books back into place. "She can't be upset over you seeing her yearbooks and some old novels. Or some cheap jewelry, for that matter. But I'll repack it. I can't do anything about the packing tape."

Clair had barely finished replacing the contents when we heard the front door bang open and my mother's footsteps in the foyer. "Hi, Liberty. I'm here."

Clair stared at me with wide eyes and mouthed,

"Wow."

I shouted, "We're in the bedroom." And my mother wasted no time finding us.

"That was quick. I didn't expect you so soon. Are you out of breath? Did you run in from the car?"

"Of course not. I'm not as young as I used to be. I'm simply out of shape and I get breathless once in a while."

Her gaze fell on Clair, sitting on the floor beside the precious package with packing tape hanging. "Hi Clair. How are you? Let me get that box out of your way."

She didn't wait for Clair's reply. Instead, she focused on me. "I see you've already opened it."

"Sorry, the tape sort of fell apart when we brought it down. Do you want to look through it now? Maybe you won't have to lug it home, and we can carry it out to the garbage can for you."

"No." Mother swooped down and snatched the box from the floor. The woman showed no signs of being out of shape. "I'll take my time going through it at my apartment and then dispose of it. It's probably nothing, but I'm feeling a little nostalgic today. This will be fun."

She pivoted and strode from the room. On her way across the threshold, Mother called, "Bye Liberty. I'll talk to you later. It was nice to see you, Clair."

I followed her to the foyer and waved from the doorway as she backed out of the drive.

When I returned to the bedroom, Clair still sat on the floor beside a pile of dried-up packing tape. She raised her eyebrows. "Katherine was in a hurry."

"That was easily the shortest visit I've ever had with my mother."

"Wasn't it strange? She seemed overly protective of an old box of books and some ancient costume jewelry.

I saw nothing of any value." Clair paused and lowered her voice. "I hate to bring up a scary subject, but her odd behavior could indicate emotional problems."

I tried to laugh but it came out as more of a hiccup. "No, she's fine. It's probably just one of those days. We all have them."

"I guess she has a right to her idiosyncrasies." Clair pushed herself up from the floor. "What's next?"

"First, help me push that ladder back up into the ceiling. Then, I'll run the vacuum in here and brew us some tea."

The attic door popped back into place with less effort, shutting off the room I'd assumed would be empty. That closed door had opened a gateway to some troubling questions. My mother seemed so protective about her past. Should I attribute it to an old woman's idiosyncrasy?

Or—could my mother be hiding some sort of secret?

Chapter Ten

Hesitating in the grocery store lot exit. I could turn left to go straight home. Or I could crank the wheel to the right and stop by my mother's apartment to return the sweater she'd left in my car a couple of weeks earlier. It was likely an overreaction, but I didn't want her to see my groceries since I'd declined her offer to shop for me only a day before. She'd been acting strange enough without hurting her feelings over her grocery shopping habits.

I convinced myself to save a trip. I would drop off her sweater. Katherine Cassell would undoubtedly be off doing her charity work at this time of day.

With her apartment key in hand, I turned the car toward Clairmont Retirement Village.

As I'd expected, her vehicle was nowhere to be seen when I claimed the nearest vacant spot in. Grabbing the sweater, I hoofed it to the building. Knocked once just to be safe. I let myself in.

"Hello?" Again, no answer. The apartment appeared neat and tidy and smelled of lavender. Floors vacuumed, gleaming coffee table. It never ceased to amaze me that anyone so busy in the community could keep a pristine house. I hung the sweater on the back of a kitchen chair, and then stood a minute longer.

Mission completed, my 'good child self' planned to leave. But fascination with the mysterious box hung over my mind like a shroud. Stored in the attic countless years and then whisked out of my hands in an instant. What would cause a woman to be so protective of an old dusty package?

My 'good child self' and that other 'self' argued. Good self: it was her business, not mine. Other self: anything affecting my mother's emotional health was indeed my business. As a responsible daughter, I had a duty to investigate.

If I was quick and careful, she'd never know I snooped. I stepped into the living room. Neat as always. Nothing out of the ordinary.

My feet led me down the hall and quietly into her bedroom. Breathing shallow, hands trembling. I half-expected her to launch from the nearest closet to catch me.

My prize was in plain view. There, on her pure white bedspread lay the dusty box she'd been so determined I not see. She hadn't thrown it or the contents into the trash can as I thought she might. The mystery novels had been tossed to the side. Two books labeled E-Town Gold lay next to one another in the middle of the bed. She'd been reminiscing. I hoped she had found some fond memories. The old jewelry was not in view but I was more interested in what the books would tell me.

Sliding onto the bed, I took care not to muss the spread and picked up the latest yearbook. I'd already seen her class photo so I leafed through other pages searching for any casual pics or telltale remarks penned by old friends.

This investigation proved disappointing. Clair and I hadn't missed anything. There was still the one impersonal note from a teacher wishing her the best of luck. I imagined it was the same as he'd written to every student in the class.

I dropped the yearbook on the bed and closed my eyes. What kind of daughter sneaked into her mother's house? I felt like a thief. I should march right back to my car and go home. And I almost did. I stood, but then reasoned the crime had already been committed. I might as well check out the other yearbook.

Did she have friends in her junior year? Settling back on the bed, I leafed to the back of that book, this time rewarded with half a dozen autographs. I supposed they were all written to my mother, even though addressed to Kat, not Katherine. Surprising, since my mother had never cared for nicknames. She'd always been adamant that I use my full name and would roll her eyes when anyone called me Lib or Libby.

As I read the notes, I wondered about that young girl called Kat.

"Kat. Thanks for showing me what real fun is. I can't wait for our next adventure!"
Joan

I tried to imagine Mother as a teenager. What was real fun to her? Could she have been adventurous?

"Kat! Thanks for making this year so exciting!! You are the best. See you at our next party. Ha. Ha.
Peggy

What did they consider exciting, back in the day?

"Kat. To the girl most likely to succeed at everything

and anything she puts her mind to."
B

I agreed with that one. When Katherine Cassell put her mind to something, she did it.

"To the life of the party."
JF

I laughed at that one. What kind of parties would they have had?

There were two names without notes.
Eddy G
Printed in small careless letters.
Gary E
Written in tiny script.
Did they have nothing to say?

I grabbed her senior yearbook for one more inspection. This would be my third trip through it, and I had to ask myself what I expected. No friendly notes had magically appeared on the back pages. No Joan or Susan or B. Why was that year different from the year before? Where did her friends go? Even if they'd had a falling out, wouldn't the girl, Kat of the previous year, have made new friends? With only first names and initials, I couldn't tell if any of them were still at Evelynton High School for senior year. One or two might have moved away. But all of them?

Clasping the books to my chest, I tried to imagine high school in the seventies.

Was I over-thinking it? Had I created a mystery that didn't exist?

Or, could there have been an automobile accident

where several friends were killed? Possible. Knowing my mother, she would never have told me about it. It would have been too distressing.

Was there trouble at home that would have caused my mother to withdraw from her social circle? There had been no divorce, and I'd never heard of a separation. My grandparents were happily married until they passed away, as far as I knew.

I pulled open the drawer of the bedside lamp table, found a notebook and tore out a page. Then I copied the names and notes I'd found in the E-Town Gold. This called for some brainstorming with Clair.

Double-checking once again, I leafed through both books. They hadn't changed, and I thought again, how I might be wanting to create a story where there was none. It was possible, even probable, that her life was exactly as she'd described it. A monotonous existence. Nothing to write about, even in her final year at Evelynton High School.

The bedside clock caught my eye. I'd been sitting in my mother's room for more than half an hour. My groceries were in the car, frozen food probably melting. Worse than that, my mother might arrive at any minute. What would I tell her if she walked in on me?

I jumped up and smoothed the bedspread, then replaced the books in as close to the original position as I could remember. I hurried out of the apartment, taking time to scan the parking lot for my mother before I climbed into my car.

As I pulled out of the lot, I picked up my cell phone and punched in a speed dial.

"Clair. I just stopped over at Mom's and checked out her school yearbooks again."

"Good. What did she say?"

"Nothing. I mean she wasn't there. I dropped off a sweater she'd left at my house and the books were on her bed. In plain sight. So, I leafed through them again looking for clues. Her friends called her Kat. Why would they do that? She hates nicknames." I continued to describe the curious notes I found. "I wrote everything down. Maybe you can get something from them that I couldn't see."

"You know the answer could be that she was too busy that day to go around collecting autographs. I admit the lack of signatures would be odd for me, but Katherine is a different person. I think it's obvious she has always been focused on her good works."

"Okay. I guess you're right. But I still don't understand the difference between her junior and senior years. I wonder if a tragedy occurred that year."

"I never heard of anything when I lived in Evelynton. I mean there was nothing big enough for people to talk about years later. I'm pretty sure I spoke to enough homeowners to be filled in on the entire history of the town." Clair paused. "Here's another thought. Being a girl, maybe it was hormonal, and she decided she didn't like anyone. Wait. More likely, knowing your mother, that's the year she discovered the library."

"You're not being much help." Or maybe she was, but I didn't want to hear the easy answer. "I better hang up. I'm at my house already, and I don't even remember driving here."

I pulled into my driveway and pushed the gear shift into park, thankful I hadn't had a wreck on the way home. Before I had a chance to climb out of the car, my phone rang. It was Clair. "I've got it. I know how we might solve this whole mystery and have fun doing it. Let's take a road trip. We'll go to Evelynton, Indiana. It isn't far. I can't believe you've never been there."

"My mother hasn't made the town sound particularly attractive. Though I admit it would be helpful to get a mental picture of the place."

"It'll be fun. I haven't had the chance to play detective since before I got married. We'll look up some of my old friends and find someone who knew your mother. Even if we don't discover anything interesting, you'll feel better. And it's about time you get to see your mom's hometown."

A dull ache snaked through my shoulder muscles, and I felt a bit short of breath. "When would we go? I'll have to make arrangements. Ask for time off. Be sure my work is caught up."

"It's only one day, Lib. Call Stanley. Tell him you will be taking a day off."

Tell him? Could I do that? "What excuse will I give?"

Clair sighed so loud I heard it through the phone. "You don't have to give Stanley an excuse. You've always been reliable. Why shouldn't you take a personal day? Choose a day next week and take it off. You're going to learn to live a little."

She made it sound easy. "Next week? I guess I can do that."

"And don't tell your mother anything. She probably won't even notice you're gone."

That caused me to swallow hard. Since my father had died, I'd always been careful not to worry my mother. But Clair was right. Mom would be so busy she probably wouldn't notice my absence. "Okay. That's smart."

"Great. Michael will be out of town all week at a convention, so the timing is perfect."

I remained quiet while I thought it over, freeing Clair to continue her encouragement. "I know you'll want to give Stanley all the particulars, but remember you don't need to explain. Give him no more information than necessary."

That afternoon, I walked into the hardware store and told Mr. Bennett I was taking a day off. And that's all I told him. It was exhilarating.

As the days passed, my anticipation grew. I would see the town that helped form my mother's personality. I might find there was no mystery, and those who remembered Katherine Baron would describe her exactly as I knew her. Hard working, law abiding, steady, unexciting.

On the other hand, I hoped the visit would unlock mysteries kept hidden from me since I'd been born. What secrets would be exposed in this visit to Evelynton, Indiana? And uppermost in my mind was one thought.

Who was…Kat?

Chapter Eleven

Woke up giddy with thoughts of the road trip and hopscotched from the bed to the bathroom. From there I skipped to the kitchen to load the coffee maker. It had been way too long since I took a trip.

Why hadn't I ever been to Evelynton? Whatever the answer, everything would be made clear in a few days. My heritage, my family history was to be revealed. There might not be much to learn, but I allowed myself the excitement of childish anticipation.

As the coffeemaker sizzled and I held my cup, misgivings began to poke holes in the wings of my frivolous dream. I pictured my mother, Katherine Cassell, kind, generous, hardworking, and loving parent. She had always been honest with me. What ungrateful daughter would choose to deceive her?

I chugged down my morning coffee and strode to the car determined to confess the sneak attack on her privacy. My plan? First, to come right out and ask her about her life, because I hadn't been clear enough in the past. I envisioned a deep mother-daughter talk. I imagined we would laugh about those tender high school years, and at that point I'd tell her about the planned trip to Evelynton.

~~

We sat in her cozy kitchen. She'd brewed tea as she always did when I came to visit. You could always count on feeling welcome and special in this place. A blessing she bestowed on anyone lucky enough to sit in her kitchen. I scooted my chair closer to her little round breakfast table and cradled my cup.

She pulled out a chair across from me, settled in, and leaned forward to look into my eyes. I knew then that she sensed this visit wasn't as casual as I pretended.

"So, tell me. What's bothering you today?"

I gulped. Suddenly feeling like a little girl who had skipped school, even though I wouldn't know how that felt-because I never had.

I jumped in. "Do you remember the other day when I found the box of your stuff in the attic? You made a point of telling me not to open it. I didn't ask why. It was your business." I paused to catch a breath. "The thing is, we had already opened it and looked in before you got there to pick it up." I was quick to add a defense before she got the wrong idea. "This was before your call, and we didn't see much. When you got there, I didn't admit it because you seemed insistent that I stay away from the contents. Didn't know why because there was nothing but a few books. But it's your possession and I understood you had your reasons.

I shrugged and gave my best innocent daughter smile. "It was silly. I probably should have told you right away."

She was quiet. This made me nervous, and I felt the need to fill the silence. "Anyway, that's my confession."

My mother took time to sip her tea before giving her noncommittal answer. "I see."

I waited, but she didn't say more. I remembered this was how she raised me and my brother. Always giving us lots of time to confess any infraction of the house rules. Patiently waiting until we spewed all.

For some reason my bangs were damp and stuck to my forehead. I swiped them off my face. "Oh, there's something else. I was here on a day when you were out—just to drop off your sweater. I happened to see the books in your bedroom." Another quick breath. "That's not true. It didn't simply happen. I looked for them."

My mother nodded. No hint of anger or disapproval.

I was sliding quickly into the guilt of a twelve-year-old truant. Where did that come from? Keep talking, Libby.

"Anyway, I couldn't get that box out of my mind. To be honest, it reminded me of how little I know about your life. For instance, I have no idea of what you liked about school, or what you didn't like. In fact, I don't know anything about your hometown.

Why didn't we ever visit Grandma and Grandpa? I remember their holiday visits, but we never went to their house. As I recall, they didn't reminisce about your childhood, either. So, tell me about your life. It's mine, too. My ancestry."

Mother closed her eyes and pulled her cup close. She began a slow shake of her head. "Silly girl. There is nothing to tell. I don't talk about those years because they were so unexciting. You would have been bored to death if you had lived my childhood."

"It can't have been that bad. I bet everyone thinks of their life as dull, but it's actually interesting to someone else, particularly the kids. What about the kids you grew up with? Who was your best friend?"

My mother shrugged and shook her head. "Nothing to tell. I was a typical introvert. I didn't have many friends of any kind. No one close enough to be called a best friend."

"You had some in your junior year." I stopped short. "Yes, I looked at the yearbooks. I saw the messages on the back pages of your junior year. But then by the senior year, there didn't seem to be any. What changed?"

"Me. I changed." She shifted in her chair to gaze out the window. "I decided it was more important to study and prepare myself for the future. Friends had either moved or simply drifted away. And once I'd settled in Twin Fawn I saw no reason to revisit Evelynton. Your grandparents loved to travel, so they were always happy to come here."

"Hmph." I pressed on. "There must have been girlfriends you kept in touch with."

My mother's sweet, patient expression faltered. "Okay. Really, Liberty, I don't know why you want to dredge up the past. I was a loner, with very few friends. Not something I'm proud of." She paused to swipe hair from her forehead. "Yes, there were girls that I ran around with in my junior year but they moved on or left town. I don't remember which. I dedicated my senior year to studying. I wanted to be prepared for college."

Suddenly, I thought about how teen girls could be cruel. Why hadn't I realized there might be painful memories.

Better to let that topic go. I altered my approach. "Well then, a boyfriend. Or someone who at least had a crush on you. I know you met Dad after you moved here. He said it was love at first sight. But who did you like in high school?"

She blew out a breath. Her tone of voice hinted that she'd lost patience with my questioning. "No one. There was no one until your father."

I stared at the woman in front of me. Could she really have been so introverted that there were no friends or boyfriends in that important last year of school? I decided yes, it might be true. I couldn't imagine her with a group of close girlfriends. At least not friends like mine.

My mother's voice grew hard as she shot the next comments at me. "I've never talked about my life because it isn't pleasant to remember. I was a disappointment to your grandparents, and I've never come to terms with it. They expected me to live up to a certain code of conduct. And I didn't." She stood and turning her back to me, moved close to the window. "I guess I'm still trying."

"Grandma and Grandpa were proud of you. I know they were. They always seemed to so happy to see you."

"I suppose they were, once I was married and had my position at the library. They thought I'd finally lived up to my potential." She whirled around and grabbed the teapot. I still couldn't see her face as she placed the pot in the sink.

Was that the punctuation ending our conversation?

I skated on thin ice, but frustration caused me to repeat. "Isn't there anything you can tell me about Evelynton? What was it like when you were growing up?"

"A sleepy little town with nothing much to do." She turned on the hot water and squirted in dish soap.

When she turned back around, her mood seemed to have changed. Her sweet smile returned, and she glanced at the clock above the stove. "Look at the time. It's so late. The library staff needs my help today. We're selling some of the old books and they can never decide which ones to let go. Promised I'd be there."

She picked up our teacups to take to the sink. Her back to me once again, she raised her voice over rushing water. "I have to run. Would you mind finishing the dishes? I don't want to be late." Before she'd finished the sentence, she'd blotted her hands on a dishtowel and taken several strides toward the door. "Bye, dear."

I turned off the hot water and stood staring at the empty doorway. What had happened? I'd always considered my mother one of the balanced people. Never flustered. Consistently certain of her purpose. Could her childhood have been so difficult? Had that little town been so deadly dull? And if it was, why not talk about it?

The teapot and cups lay in the sudsy water. I finished washing and put them away.

Before I left my mother's apartment, I couldn't resist another stroll into her bedroom. All neat and tidy. No sign of the box from the attic. The closet door was not quite closed so I took a couple quick steps and jerked it open. Nothing out of the ordinary. Her clothing hung in orderly rows, sorted by color. The floor was bare except for one pair of sensible shoes.

I closed the closet door and took my time leaving the apartment, scanning each room on my way out. Everything in its place. So typical of my mother. One picture of my grandparents hung on the wall. A couple pictures of Chad and his family, from a visit to the lake last summer, sat on the bookshelf next to one of me. It had been snapped on my last birthday when Mom took me out to dinner. There was nothing to hint at any secrets she held close.

Questions cycled through my head. If she'd really experienced such an uneventful life, why wouldn't she talk about it, if only to complain?

I pulled the apartment door closed and the thought hit me. I hadn't mentioned the road trip to Evelynton. Given Mother's reaction to my probe, maybe that was a secret I should keep.

Chapter Twelve

The day of the road trip had finally arrived. Mysterious Hoosier town or deadly dull hamlet. Which would it be?

In the three days since my failed attempt in extracting information, I'd let our relationship return to normal, pretending nothing had happened. My mother and I met as often as we always had, but I stuck to safe topics. She seemed relieved and avoided long conversations.

Silencing the ringer on my cell phone on that brisk morning hadn't helped. The phone vibrated across the bedside table making me nervous while I got prepared for the trip. As a good mother, I knew she would continue to call, eventually phoning the police if I didn't pick up.

I threw up my hands reasoning I could get through one more conversation. The one tug at my confidence being my family's all-important principle—*Good children don't lie.* Drilled into me from the time I could form sentences. This followed by the Cassell family precept—*If you can't tell it to your mother, it must be wrong.*

I answered the phone, put on a smile, and asked about her plans for the day. In the midst of the usual chatter, I told her about my day off. Clair and I would be spending the day together, maybe taking a drive. I cut it short at that. No lies, no deceit.

No confession needed, even though the words had been coursing through my veins. I stopped short of blurting the whole ugly truth. *Yes, Mother. Clair and I are going to your hometown to snoop. Since you won't tell me anything, we will find people who knew you and make inquiries about your sordid past.* I breathed easier.

I understood that many people, and definitely my friend Clair, would wonder why I felt the obligation to divulge as much as I did. But anything less would have vexed me all day. Fortunately, Mom's interest stopped short of forcing me to fabricate a story.

~~

When I stepped out onto the porch, the morning haze still hovered over Twin Fawn, and the birds were in the midst of their early morning chatter. My ride—Clair in her BMW—arrived at seven a.m. sharp. The perfect hostess/chauffeur, she handed me a Mocha Latte and a bakery sack.

I settled into the soft leather seat and peeked into the bag. "Scones. This makes rolling out of bed worthwhile."

"Fasten your seat belt." Clair slid her own coffee into the cup holder and guided the car onto the street.

I savored a few slurps of the creamy hot mocha and gazed out the window, intending to enjoy the scenery, now racing by at a good clip. "Um, how long will we be on the road?"

"It usually takes about three and a half hours, but if we get ahead of the traffic on the interstate, maybe three."

As soon as we moved into the flow of early morning commuters, Clair picked up her cup and sipped. "I'm still wrapping my mind around the fact that this is your first trip to Evelynton. It isn't far away."

"I've been wondering the same. When I was growing up, if my mother spoke of Evelynton at all, it was short, and I got the feeling that she'd rather not." I paused to consider what I'd said. "You know those silent signals you get as a child? The parent doesn't have to say a thing. You just know."

Clair glanced at me and scrunched her eyebrows. "Yes. I guess I know what you mean, although there wasn't much my parents wouldn't talk about. It beats me why Evelynton would be on the banned subject list. It isn't exactly a destination vacation spot, but it's okay."

She replaced her coffee and pressed on the gas pedal to pass a truck. "Well, you're going to see it now. Better late than never."

I clutched the armrest to steady myself at the change in velocity. "What if I find out something horrible about my family?"

"Something horrible? Think about who we're talking about. Katherine Cassell, librarian, pillar of the community." Clair took her eyes off the road long enough to grin at me.

Becoming more serious, she continued. "You're certainly old enough to know your family history. If there is sadness there, you can help her deal with it.

"You're right. It's time she understood that I'm not a fragile little girl. I can handle anything." I inspected my shirt and brushed crumbs onto the floor, then glanced at Clair. "Sorry. I'll vacuum your car for you when we get home."

"But the most likely story is Mom was telling the truth when she said her life was too tedious to warrant discussion. And I've been worrying over nothing." I shrugged and pulled a second scone from the bag.

We settled into companionable silence for the remainder of the trip. I drank my coffee and polished off the rest of the scones. Before I knew it, we had veered off the interstate and were driving north. My imagination sparked to life again as we drew closer to Evelynton. Nerves made it difficult to sit still. After all the secrecy, I was about to see where my mother grew up. The infamous, or possibly the colorless, Evelynton, Indiana.

We passed the city limit sign, and I sat forward in my seat to absorb the sights. Sort of a disappointment. Mom was right. I saw nothing notable about the little burg. No grand houses. Nothing in the least bit interesting. Lifeless neighborhoods. Not even the spooky historical buildings I'd imagined over the years.

"I know where your grandparents lived, so let's drive by." Clair took a few turns and slowed as we passed a gray two-story house, drab and in need of repair. Overgrown shrubs and tricycles in the yard. "Of course, it sold after they passed. I don't know who lives there now. We could stop and ask if they would let you see the inside."

"No. I don't think so. I'm pretty sure I was never there, even as a toddler. It doesn't bring back any memories."

We drove on. As we cruised the narrow streets, I tried to imagine my mother as a fifteen-year-old schoolgirl. Would she have walked past these homes with a group of girl friends? Laughing? Talking about boys? Maybe not.

Clair interrupted my thoughts. "Our first stop will be

to see my friend Rarity. She's been a hairdresser for years and knows practically everyone in town. All the town gossip eventually makes its way into her shop. The tough part is convincing her to share what she hears."

I grabbed the armrest to keep from sliding against Clair as she made a sharp right turn into a parking lot. We snagged a spot near the front.

My friend threw open the car door and hopped out, pointing to a square red-brick building across the street. The wide window in the front displayed a large poster of curly hair with the salon name, The Rare Curl, splashed across it.

Clair hurried to the curb and stood with outstretched arms. "There it is. I've missed Rarity and her haircuts. Wait until you meet this woman. You'll love her."

"Hold on. I'm coming." I picked up the pace to join my friend in stepping off the curb and into the street.

She continued raving about the beloved hairdresser as we dodged traffic. "There's nobody nicer in town. Or wiser. She encouraged me to give Michael a chance when he asked me out. I didn't think he was my style, but she knew."

A blaring horn from an old rusty pickup truck encouraged us to move out of the road. "I've been so busy since we relocated, there hasn't been time to keep in touch. I can't wait to see her."

Having safely reached our destination, we pushed through the door of The Rare Curl. Tinkling bells alerted the woman at the reception desk of our arrival. She raised green eyes and flashed a radiant smile. Pushing a mass of auburn curls from her face she sang out. "Clair Lane!" Her chair slid back and she scurried over to wrap my friend in a hug. "Oh sorry. It's Clair Berry, now. How could I forget? I'm so glad to see you. How's that handsome husband of yours?" She leaned to the side to peer through the window. "Is he here with you?"

Clair laughed and put her hands on the woman's shoulders. "Slow down, Rarity. Michael's not with me this trip. But this is my friend from Twin Fawn, Libby Cassell. Her mother grew up in Evelynton." And then, I experienced Rarity's introductory hug.

When Rarity released me, Clair continued. "I'm showing Libby around town. She's never visited and we decided it was time she saw the place. And possibly get an idea of what her mother's life was like while she lived here. Her mom's name was Katherine Baron. I told Lib if anyone could tell us about Katherine it would be you. Do you remember her? We're hoping some of her old friends might be still in town."

Rarity tipped her head back and laughed. "You're right. I know just about everyone in town. I do remember Katherine Baron."

Rarity gasped and grabbed my hand. "Oh, did she pass away? I'm so sorry for your loss."

"No." I shook my head. "No, she's fine. It's just that she won't talk about her youth. You probably think I should know at least something about it, but I don't."

Rarity continued to hold my hand while I explained. "I saw my grandparents on holidays and my birthday. They always came to Twin Fawn to see us, but they never talked about the past. And neither did my mother. I didn't think it was strange at the time. But Clair has made me aware that most people know at least something of their family history."

Rarity pressed her lips together for a moment. "Katherine's life here? Maybe that's your mother's story to tell. I don't think I should be talking about her."

I sucked in a breath. "Oh please. It's just that as she gets older, she sometimes acts sort of strange and forgets things. I'm hoping that learning about her past will help me understand how to help her."

Rarity's eyes widened and she nodded. "Oh my. I see."

Okay, should I feel guilty? Why had I given the impression my mother suffered from dementia? She didn't. Or I hoped not. I clamped my mouth shut before I admitted the exaggeration. Still anxious for all the information I could get.

Rarity put an index finger to her chin. "I understand your feelings. I doubt I know anything about Katherine that isn't already public knowledge, so I guess it's okay. I'll tell you what I remember."

"Let's sit down." Rarity led us to seats in the salon waiting area. "You arrived at the perfect time. I'm not expecting anyone for a while."

The hairdresser clasped her hands and leaned toward me. "Katherine, Kat as we called her, was a class or two ahead of me, so I didn't know her well. But I saw her around the school. She was such a pretty girl." Rarity leaned back to gaze at me. "You look like her."

Clair settled in a chair beside Rarity. "What can you tell us?"

"Let's see, what do I remember?" Rarity tapped her forehead. "Oh yes, Kat's parents were Clive and Murine Baron. They lived down on Stoneybridge Drive, only a couple of doors from where I live now. They were such a nice couple. And so interesting. They've been gone a number of years, now." Rarity turned to me and chuckled. "Well of course, you know that."

Clair leaned forward. "Describe them to Libby. I know who they were because they used to live beside my friend Lauren, but nothing else."

Rarity nodded. "Of course, it was long after Kat left home so I didn't know them as parents. And I only met Clive once or twice. I remember he was a big man. Kind of gruff." She brightened. "Murine came into the salon occasionally. Stacey cut her hair. She had such a sweet temperament."

The hairdresser smiled and gave her curls a shake. "There were some people who thought Clive and Murine were a little strange, especially when Murine was determined to learn to shoot. I was told they had a big shotgun in the house, kept next to the door. From the stories, that thing was almost as big as Murine."

She chuckled. "I can't imagine. But lots of people feel safer with some form of protection in the home, don't you think?"

We nodded. I was thinking this was new information and how happy it made me that they never brought the shotgun along on holiday visits.

Rarity paused for a moment before continuing. "Everyone is unique in God's economy, and everybody has their own way of living. That's what makes life interesting, isn't it?"

I smiled at this woman who seemed to think of only the best in people. "Pretend I'm not Katherine's daughter. What comes to mind about her? What can you tell me?"

"Let me think about it. I'm sorry the memories escape me. It seems that you would know everything that I do."

"I realize it's weird, but as I mentioned, I want to

improve our relationship."

Rarity brightened. "Oh yes. I can see her in my mind's eye. Being younger, I always envied Kat Barron. I thought of her as being very stylish. Sort of daring. She wore pretty clothes, sometimes in bright, clashing colors." I stole a glance at Clair who raised her eyebrows at me.

Rarity continued. "Some of my friends didn't understand it, but I was conscious of style choices even back then. I guess that's what brought me into hairdressing."

A frown found its way to Rarity's face. "There was some kind of shake-up at the school. I don't know if it was her class. Those of us who were younger were kept in the dark about those things. I doubt Kat had anything to do with it. Probably wasn't even anyone in her class."

Rarity paused. "I don't remember your mother in the year she graduated. It's strange because we all looked up to the seniors." She wiggled fingers at me. "Not all of them obviously, but the trendy ones."

Red curls bounced as Rarity tipped her head back and laughed. "Those were formative years. I might have started idolizing someone else. Maybe a movie star or a singer."

I couldn't help but grin at finally getting a picture, if vague, of my mother. Trendy? Stylish? "This is helpful. Do you remember any of her school friends? Maybe someone who might still live here in Evelynton?"

The hairdresser pushed a stray curl from her face. "Now you're taxing my memory. I can't think of anyone."

Clair opened her purse and pulled out the list I'd given her. "Lib and I found a few clues in Katherine's yearbook. These are people who signed it and wrote notes to her in her junior year. I'm afraid we don't have any last names."

Rarity squinted at the list in Clair's hand and shook her head. "Let me think."

I asked the question that had bothered me from the beginning and seemed to connect to her memories. "In her senior year, we didn't find any autographs. I couldn't imagine why that would be, but maybe if we find someone on this list, we can go from there." I pointed at the first signature. Only initials.

Rarity's eyes opened wide. "Oh, JF must be James Farlow. It seems that I might have seen them together occasionally." Rarity glanced at Clair and laughed. "Not the Jimmy Farlow you know. Not the policeman. This would have been his father. I remember that he, the father, got into a little trouble in high school. I don't know what it was about. Something trivial, I suppose. But that may be the reason he encouraged his son to go into law enforcement. That happens. We learn from our mistakes and try to guide our children in a better direction."

Rarity paused. "I remember James went to work in a factory after high school. It seems to me he retired and moved to Florida with his wife."

She leaned in to look at the next listing. "B? No idea there. Gary? No. Eddy? No. I don't know them either. I'm sorry I'm not being much help."

Clair studied her notebook. "That's okay. We'll find someone you do remember. What about Joan?"

Rarity squinted. "No. No one comes to mind." She paused. "Oh, there was a sad case some years ago. I'm pretty sure the woman's name was Joan, but I don't remember her last name. She wasn't in high school. It was probably someone completely different."

I pointed at the next name on the list. "How about a girl named Peggy?"

"That's a common name. There were a lot of girls named Peggy," Rarity leaned back in her chair and crossed her arms. "I wonder if it is Peggy Larkin. I remember her being about Katherine's age. Larkin is her married name. I can't remember her maiden name. But I rarely forget a face. I'm a visual person, so pictures would spark my memory. Did you bring the yearbook?"

I shook my head. "Unfortunately, we only have the notes we took. I had to leave the yearbook in Twin Fawn." I hoped Rarity wouldn't ask why. I was invading my mother's privacy enough and didn't want to confess it.

Rarity brightened. "There's always the library. Why don't you go there and get them? I'm sure they have the whole collection of E-Town Golds."

Clair grinned. "That's a great idea. Why didn't we think of it? We'll shoot over to the library and pick one up."

Clair and I hopped up and were on our way to the door when Rarity called. "Wait. Clair, do you still have a library card from Evelynton?"

My friend slumped. "Crap. No, I don't."

Rarity pivoted and scurried behind the reception desk. "Not to worry. I'll send my card with you and call to let Gloria know you have my permission to use it. Gloria is still the librarian. She'll be glad to see you."

As Rarity tapped in the phone number, she said, "You'll need the years when Katherine would have been a junior and senior, correct?"

We nodded.

"I'll ask her to pull them out so you won't have to search. And I'll let her know you're picking up the books for me. Um. What years are we talking about? I'm not sure if she was two or three years ahead of me in school."

Clair pulled out her notebook once again. " '71 and '72."

I spun and raced out the door ahead of Clair.

My mother trendy? My grandmother with a shotgun? There were answers in this town that I needed to find.

Chapter Thirteen

The library door swept open, and I hesitated a moment, taking in the book-laden shelves. Memories surfaced of the many hours spent studying in the Twin Fawn Library while I waited for my mother to finish work. Murmurs drifted my way from the people in the aisles hunched over publications and seated around tables. The peaceful sanctitude of the room shattered when Clair spotted her friend. "Gloria!"

Heads shot up and wide eyes stared at us. I returned what I hoped was an apologetic smile, and mouthed, "Sorry." They soon returned to their studies. Except the woman at the circulation desk. A grin spread across her face and she hurried to welcome Clair with a hug.

"Clair Lane Berry." The woman's hearty voice echoed from the high ceilings of the old building. "It's good to see you. How's married life?" She glanced at the library patrons with the same apologetic smile and shrugged.

After being released from Gloria's arms, Clair introduced me. I'd been eyeing Gloria's attire, but pulled my attention away long enough to nod at the woman. She grabbed my hands and gave me a hearty, but quieter greeting. All I could think to say was, "Great cowboy boots." The teal leather complimented her fringy Western vest.

Gloria leaned in. "I wear them all the time. They're so comfortable."

After a few minutes of polite, quiet conversation concerning Clair and Michael's move to Twin Fawn, Clair steered Gloria's attention to the reason for the visit.

"Oh. Of course." Gloria twisted and grabbed two E-Town Golds from her desk. "I dug these out for you and even ran a dust rag over them." She did a bit more dusting with her hand. "They aren't among the most popular of our offerings."

With yearbooks under my arm, we made our way to the door. But not before Gloria repeated the hugs and extracted a promise from Clair for a return visit.

Why hadn't my mother loved this town? While descending the old stone steps, I vowed if ever I chose to relocate, Evelynton would be the place.

We hustled back to the car and returned to The Rare Curl. I opened the passenger door before Clair had turned off the ignition. "I can't wait to see if these spark any memories."

This time, when we entered the salon, a customer occupied Rarity's chair. A wave of disappointment and impatience swept over me until our hairdresser friend waved her hairbrush at us. "Bring those books over here. Gladys won't mind if I take a minute. I just finished telling her you were in town."

Gladys, Clair, and I looked on while Rarity leafed through the pages of Katherine's junior year. Holding out the book, she pointed to a photo. "Look, Clair. This is James Farlow."

Clair pulled the book close and giggled. "Jimmy's

the image of his father."

"Aww. He is, isn't he." Rarity nodded.

She flipped more pages. "There's more than one Joan. Last names Allhouse and Crandall." She shook her head. "I don't recall anything about either of them."

Rarity continued studying the photos, then slapped a hand on a page. "I recognize these boys. They're bound to be the Gary and Eddy who signed at the back. I remember they used to hang out together." She laughed. "How could I forget them? I used to recite their names together and thought it was so funny. Gary Edwards and Eddy Garrison." Another giggle slipped out. "I wonder what happened to them. I haven't seen them in years."

Our redheaded friend continued scanning photos, eventually poking a finger at one. "I was right when I mentioned Peggy Larkin. Margaret Clooney in the yearbook. You know how Peggy is sometimes a nickname for Margaret? And Larkin is her married name. I bet she's the Peggy who signed the back. Her uncle was the insurance man who was found murdered a few years back. You remember, don't you Clair?"

"Sure do." She glanced at the woman in Rarity's styling chair. "Gladys, didn't you discover the body?"

Gladys put her hand to her mouth. "Yes, ma'am. Let me tell you, that's something I'll never forget."

Clair glanced at me. "Evelynton's first murder as far back as anyone could remember. Gladys went in to clean the insurance office early that morning and found the body."

Gladys' eyes grew wide. "I walked in, loaded with cleaning supplies, and tripped over him. Landed on the floor right beside him!"

"There was really a murder in this sweet little

village?"

Clair sighed. "A terrible thing. I'll tell you the story some time."

Rarity shook her head. "I'm sorry you were reminded of that awful time, Gladys."

To me she said, "It was such a sad day for our town. Anyway, to get back on track." She laid a finger on the photo. "This is Peggy and as I remember, she and Kat were friends."

"I would love to talk to her. Is she still around?"

"Yes, she is. She works part-time at Barbara's dress shop, just down the street. You know the place, Clair. It used to be Patricia's, but she sold it last year."

We said our goodbyes to Rarity and Gladys and set out for Barbara's Dress Shop. Located within easy walking distance, the store stood out with its window display of colorful clothing, hats and handbags. There seemed to be only one salesclerk in the building, and she directed her attention to another customer. I guessed the clerk to be closer to my age than my mother's, so not the woman we sought. My patience was tested while she consulted with a customer.

While waiting, Clair and I browsed the racks. Clair exclaimed over the bargain prices while I wondered about the benefits of updating my wardrobe.

When the customer walked out with her purchases, I approached the counter and inquired about Peggy.

"I'm sorry, Peg is off today. She won't be in again until Friday. I'm Barbara and will be happy to take care of your shopping needs. What can I help you with?"

"Thank you. It's a personal matter. We're from out of town—only here today—and I'm anxious to talk to her. Can you tell me where she lives or how to get in touch with her?"

I knew I'd asked the wrong question when she drew her head back and appraised me with narrowed eyes. "Oh, no. I would never give out an employee's private information."

I scrambled for a persuasive reply. How would I gain her trust? A furtive glance toward the sales floor confirmed my sidekick fully engrossed in shopping while I stammered. Finally, Clair's eyes met mine and she pulled herself away from the new fall collection.

As a realtor she had mastered persuasive technique and approached Barbara as if she'd known her for years. "You are wise to be cautious these days. It's shameful the way some people abuse trust. You can't be giving out information to strangers." Clair introduced herself, explaining she wasn't an actual stranger, dropping Rarity's and Gloria's names. She went on to explain she had returned for a visit. "I wonder if you might phone Peg and let her know we're here to ask about an old friend of hers. Kat Baron. Tell her we'd love to buy her a cup of coffee, if she's available."

The clerk looked dubious, but went to the phone and made the call. She glanced in our direction several times during the conversation. I thought she might be describing us. *Tall thin professional woman, dark spikey hair, dressed in high heels and an expensive suit. And shorter woman, average build, wearing blue jeans, long sleaved T-shirt, and sneakers. May be homeless.*

After a few agonizing minutes, during which I tried to stand up straighter and suck in my stomach, the clerk replaced the phone.

"Peg said she would meet you at Ava's Java Too in twenty minutes. She will be wearing a green jacket."

Clair grinned. "Great. I was hoping to stop there. Is it still wonderful?"

The salesclerk smiled and returned to the sales counter.

Clair turned to me. "Wait until you see it. Ava's Java was my favorite haunt when I lived here. I used it as my second office. It's under new management and they changed the name to Ava's Java Too. I hope they've maintained the same cozy atmosphere." She winked at me. "If they're using Ava's recipes, you'll swoon for the mocha latte."

On our way out of the dress shop, Clair called to the salesclerk, "Love your selection." and waved good-bye.

We took our time walking to Ava's Java Too, only three doors away from the dress shop. I spent the stroll counting the pedestrians who nodded and smiled as we passed. I loved this little town.

As soon as Clair pushed through the coffee shop door, we were engulfed in the powerful essence of fresh ground coffee. She twisted toward me. "Breathe that in. Isn't it heavenly?"

We picked up coffee at the counter and I turned to search for a table, but Clair seemed determined to get a particular seat. She grabbed my arm and pulled me toward the window. "This was my favorite spot. I met with my friends, Lauren and Anita, four or five times a week." She gazed around the room. "The new owners haven't changed a thing. It's perfect."

I sipped my coffee and entertained myself with people watching, only distracted when the door opened. I searched each new arrival for a green jacket and was finally rewarded, but not by the woman I'd expected. I'd pictured someone of my mother's age and stature, and with similar energy. This woman appeared older. She walked slowly, with a slight limp. Lines around her eyes might have begun life as laugh lines but appeared closer to a roadmap caused by fatigue.

The woman hesitated beside the coffee counter and Clair hopped up and rushed to pay. "Let me do this. I'm so grateful you agreed to meet us."

The woman smiled, nodded at Clair and then at me. "Thank you, that's nice. You match Barbara's description."

As soon as Peg sat, and we introduced ourselves, she said, "I was told this is about Kat Baron. Haven't heard that name in years. How is she?"

I wanted to cheer. Finally, I'd found someone who knew my mother. "She's my mom and she's fine." I proceeded to explain my interest in her youth, while avoiding the misdiagnosis of dementia. "I thought it would be helpful to speak to some of her school friends."

She placed her hands around her mug. "I'm glad she's okay. Although I'm not sure we could be described as friends. Earlier years maybe, but not at the end."

"That's the reason I'm here. I need to know what changed things. I feel that something must have happened, but she won't give me any information. Would you tell me about her?"

Peggy didn't seem to share Rarity's reluctance to spread gossip. "Sure, I'll tell you about Kat. She was a flirt. And she was cute, so she could have anyone she set her sights on. It didn't matter whose boyfriend he was." Peggy rolled her eyes and sipped coffee.

"Don't get me wrong. We got along alright. She could be fun as long as she got her way." Peggy set her coffee mug on the table and stared out the window. "That girl wouldn't let up until things went the way she wanted."

After a moment's pause, she retrieved her mug and continued. "When it came to school, Kat was smart, so she never had to study to get good grades. I wasn't so blessed. Things didn't go well for me. Kat was always thinking of things we could do instead of homework. She even talked me into skipping school." Peg leaned back in her chair and shook her head. "I followed her around like a puppy." Peggy drank her coffee and continued to gaze through the window. "I only graduated by sheer luck."

I could barely sit still, listening to the woman's lies. Why did she hold such a grudge?

Still, I wanted as much information as I could gather, so I remained calm. "We saw your autograph in Kat's 1971 yearbook, but not in 1972. Why didn't you sign that year? In my senior year everyone wanted to sign yearbooks."

Peggy glanced sideways at me. "Well, I didn't see much of her during that last year of school."

Clair rested her elbows on the table. "Why was that?"

Peggy answered while she twisted and scanned the room. "Oh, I don't know." She shrugged and spat out, "Nothing happened. You know how kids change. We drifted apart."

I lifted Clair's notebook. "We saw a signature of someone named Joan. Do you know who that is?"

The woman shot out a response. "No."

She took a breath and deflated a little as she blew it out. "Alright, yes I knew Joan. Joan Crandall died about ten years ago from an overdose. She started using drugs right after graduation." Peggy dipped her head and stared at her hands.

I almost reached out to take her hand but pulled back. "I'm so sorry about your friend. That's terrible."

The coffee began to unsettle my stomach. I hadn't considered that teenagers of my mother's time might have faced serious problems. Still, since she'd given what I knew to be a false description of my mother, how much of Peggy's story could I believe?

I determined not to expose her lies, just yet. I needed as much information as she would supply. I would sort it out later. "What about Kat's parents. My grandparents. Did you know Clive and Murine Baron? You must have spent some time at their home."

Peggy showed some relief at the change of subject. "I may have met them. We didn't pay much attention to parents, then. I might have been at the house once or twice. Our group usually met at the park or at the drug store lunch counter."

"What were my grandparents like? Were they nice? I only saw them when they visited for holidays. They passed away while I was young."

"I guess they were nice enough. Like I said, I don't remember much about them. We didn't waste time talking to the parents."

I'd reached a dead-end and searched for another subject. "As far as I know, my mother didn't come back for reunions, or anything else for that matter. Do you remember her visiting Evelynton after graduation?"

"No. I never saw her again. But I wouldn't have gone to a reunion, so how would I know if she showed up or not?"

Clair interjected. "Oh, one more question. Do you have any idea who B might be?" She gave a short laugh.

"I know it's a stretch. What can you tell from one initial? But that's all we have to go on. Did any of your friends go by B?"

Peggy stared at Clair without expression. "No idea."

"Okay, just a couple more questions." Clair picked up her notebook. "Do you know Gary Edwards or Eddy Garrison? We were told they were friends of Kat."

Peggy fidgeted and glanced around the room. "No."

Peggy had changed her tune once before, so I probed. "They would have been in your class. We were hoping they were still in town and we might contact them."

She blew out a breath. "They were, but I didn't know them well. You won't find them. They both left town years ago."

Clair jumped in. "Why did they leave?"

"How would I know? A better question is why anybody stayed in this town. Nothing ever happened here."

From Peggy's hostility, it was clear this woman held something back. A change of subject might keep her talking. "Do you have any idea of why my mother wouldn't want me to visit Evelynton?"

Peggy straightened in her chair and gazed out the window. She only glanced at us when she shook her head, but as she did, I saw her expression had changed from fatigue to anger. "No. I don't know anything about that. We didn't keep in touch. I shouldn't even be talking to you since I didn't really know her. It is best to live in the present. Why rake over the garbage of the past?"

She lifted her coffee mug in both hands and tipped it up, downing the last dregs. "I can't tell you anymore. Kat Baron and I were casual acquaintances. I haven't seen her in years and don't know anything about her. It seems to me that if she wouldn't tell you about those years, there was a reason." Peggy pushed her chair from the table and stood.

Clair jumped up. "Take my business card. If you remember anything, would you please call me? We would really appreciate anything you can tell us."

"I won't. There's nothing more to remember." But she accepted the card and slid it into her pocket.

"Thanks for buying. It's the only reason I agreed to meet you. I never get good coffee anymore"

We were left sputtering as she spun away from the table and paced to the door.

I watched through the window as Peggy blended into the crowd of people on the street and was gone.

Clair stared at me wide eyed. "What's that all about?"

I just shook my head. "She's a deeply troubled woman. I'm not sure I believe anything she said."

Instead of becoming clear, the view into my mother's past had grown foggy, causing me to question if it would be worth digging any deeper.

Chapter Fourteen

I leaned against the brick wall outside Ava's Java Too while Clair answered her cell phone. The softening of her voice and fond comments hinted she spoke to her husband. I tried not to listen in, occupying my time searching the solemn faces of passing Evelynton citizens. Where had the friendly smiles gone? None of these people appeared huggable.

Clair ended the call. "Michael's between meetings and wanted to check in. He's having a good time and...." She leveled her gaze at me. "But I see you're not. Don't let one unhappy woman wreck your day. I don't believe that stuff she said about Katherine, do you?"

"Not a word. Nothing she said sounded like my mother. She's let her own emotional issues color her memory. Or maybe she fabricated a story to get free coffee."

Clair pocketed her phone and checked her watch. "I wish we had connected with more of Katherine's friends."

"That would have been helpful." I gazed down the street, taking in the dress shop, Ava's Java Too and The Rare Curl. Still quaint and inviting. "But at least I've seen Evelynton."

Clair glanced toward the parking lot. "There's a hamburger stand at the edge of town. Let's pick up a sandwich on the way out of town."

I prepared to follow Clair to the car, but she stopped and pivoted to face me. "Wait. There's one more person we should talk to. It's a long shot, and he might not be willing to give us any time at all. But since we're here, we might as well cover all bases."

She began a fast stride down the sidewalk. "Follow me. We're going to that block building on the next corner."

"Hold on." I skidded to a stop after reading the sign above the door. "Why are we going to the police station? Do you really think there might be something in the police records about my mother? That's crazier than Peggy's stories."

Clair twisted to face me. "I'm not saying Katherine has any kind of police record. But do you remember when Rarity pointed out the picture of James Farlow? She thought he was probably a friend of your mother's. His son, Jimmy, is a policeman."

"Oh. So, we're going to ask about his dad, not my mother?"

"Yes. Jimmy might know something about the friendship between his dad and Katherine. He might even be able to name more of their friends."

"Wonderful." My attitude improved and I picked up the pace again.

Clair maintained a narrative as we walked. "I'll warn you. Meeting with Jimmy won't be your idea of fun. Even if he knows something that will help us, he might not share it. And to be honest, Jimmy isn't the easiest person to communicate with on his good days. I can't tell you how many times he wanted to arrest me."

I applied the brakes, again. "What do you mean, arrest you? What did you do?"

"Nothing, really. I might have been in the wrong place at the wrong time. He never succeeded because my friends and I never did anything wrong."

I planted my fists on my hips. "Great. So, why do you think we should talk to him?"

My friend, who had been several strides ahead, retraced her steps. "I'm sorry about the poor introduction. But I didn't want you to be surprised, should he prove difficult. But it's possible James Farlow, senior, mentioned something about his time in high school, and we might be able to pry it out of Jimmy."

Clair smiled. "The truth is I sort of miss Jimmy Farlow. I'd like to see him. For better or for worse, he is part of this town." She grabbed my arm and continued the trek. "Come on."

My friend Clair tended to be a fast walker, even in high heels. By the time we arrived, I leaned on the railing to catch my breath. Then I assessed the stone stairs in front of me. "It's an impressive building. Why are the steps so high?" Each step appeared to be about two inches higher than necessary.

"That's one of the town oddities. I've always thought the founding fathers wanted people to be intimidated when entering. That way the police would command more respect."

"Anyone who climbs those stairs everyday gets my respect." I bypassed the steps and took the wheelchair ramp. Clair, who of course scaled the stairs, held the door for me when I met her at the top.

The officer manning the reception desk didn't seem

particularly intimidating. Clair strutted past him, taking the hallway to our left while he dipped a donut into a cup of coffee.

I tagged after her, giving him a weak smile and a small wave.

Clair came to a halt at the first door, causing me to slam on the brakes to avoid bumping into her. After a quick tap on the door, she proceeded without waiting for an answer. The man inside jerked his head up and pushed away from the desk, shoving his chair back. He stood ramrod straight and I couldn't help but admire his perfectly pressed uniform. I wondered how could anyone remain wrinkle free while manning a desk? How much starch would it require?

The officer didn't acknowledge me as I slid in beside Clair but shot her with a glare. "Mrs. Berry. What brings you to our city?"

"Hi, Jimmy. How nice of you to remember me. May we come in? If you have a few minutes, my friend Libby Cassell has some questions."

"Libby, this is Jimmy Farlow."

He sighed. "It's Officer Farlow, if you don't mind. And it looks as though you're already in." He motioned to the two chairs facing his desk and returned to his seat.

I kept my head down and lowered myself into the closest chair. The man made me nervous and caused my mind to swirl, while I tried to decide how to begin. I sneaked a glance at Clair, hoping she would jump in and take the lead.

Clair relaxed in her chair and crossed her legs. Farlow gazed at her for a moment. Then he turned his frigid stare on me. "Yes?"

So, Clair was leaving it to me after all. I took a breath.

Words and syllables tumbled from my mouth. I hoped they came out in some sort of order that made sense. He didn't seem like a man who put up with confusion.

When I'd finished, he blinked at me. "I don't know what you expect me to tell you. You said your mother left town after her high school graduation, so obviously it was long before my time. I never met Katherine Baron and if my father knew the woman, he didn't tell me about it. Why would he?" The officer picked up a few papers from his desk and began shuffling them.

Thankfully, Clair jumped in to clarify my disheveled presentation. "I realize this is a long shot but we don't know where else to turn. Maybe you can tell us about your dad. We know he was a friend of Kat's."

Officer Farlow breathed out a long breath, gazed at me and gestured toward Clair. "I don't know you, but I've dealt with Mrs. Berry in the past. It's been her habit to pester me to death. If you're anything like her other friends, you'll do the same. Let's get to the point. What do you want to know?"

I smiled at him, pretending he didn't scare me. "Would you tell me about what your father was like as a young person? I thought it might help us to understand my mother, having grown up at the same time. Did he aspire to become a policeman like you?"

Farlow sighed. "No, that wasn't his goal, although he had the integrity for it."

Clair leaned forward and softened her voice. "We heard he might have run into a little trouble with the law. Is that true?"

Jimmy Farlow shot out of his chair. I braced myself in case he leapt across the desk. "Of course, it's not true. Who have you been talking to?"

Officer Farlow smoothed his shirt and took a breath. "My father was strait-laced. Made sure I always obeyed the rules. He wouldn't suffer a wrinkle on my shirt, much less any infraction of the law. He's the reason I chose a career in law enforcement. He respected the brotherhood, and I'm proud to be his son."

Clair hadn't handled that well. I took over. "Please forgive us. It was something we heard, and if we hear such malicious gossip again, we'll certainly clear it up."

I smiled my best peaceful smile. "Let's move on. Did he enjoy his time in high school?"

Farlow slowly lowered himself into his chair. He stared at me and then at Clair. Then shifted his attention to me again. "Did he enjoy it? He never spoke of his schooling, but he was very concerned with my education. He stayed in the present, not the past."

Clair jumped in. "Did he give you the impression that he liked school? What were his favorite subjects?"

Farlow closed his eyes for a moment. "I don't know. He never said. I repeat, he did not talk about the past."

The officer leaned forward with his elbows on the desk. It was as relaxed as I'd seen him since we sat down. "Listen. Men don't chit-chat like you women do. We don't feel the need to share every little emotion."

With that, he grabbed the stack of papers from his desk and straightened them. "Obviously, I can't help you with your inquiry. Now, if you'll excuse me, I have some police work to do."

I took the not-so-subtle hint and stood, but Clair put up a hand. "One more thing. What do you know about a woman named Joan Crandall? Apparently, she was once a friend of Katharine's. We heard she died of a drug overdose about ten years ago. I imagine she would have known your father as well."

"Drug overdose? I remember it. It was before my parents moved south. My father knew of her but didn't supply any pertinent information." The man's cheeks were turning red, but I thought he should be commended for controlling his temper.

"Was she a known drug user? Do you remember any of her friends?"

Jimmy shook his head. His voice gradually increasing in volume. "Do you know how many cases come across my desk in a day?"

I wanted to answer that there couldn't be many in this small town, but I kept quiet.

"What's more, you're asking about a police matter. It's nothing I would discuss with you."

He slammed the stack of papers onto the desk. "You may leave."

Clair persevered. "One more question. What about Gary Edwards or Eddy Garrison?"

Farlow stared at her. "Now you're playing games. Get out."

"No, they're real people."

Farlow grabbed the papers from his desk once again. I prepared to duck in the event that he threw them at us.

Ever persistent Clair picked up the pace of her questioning. "And there was someone with the initial B." Officer Farlow glared at Clair, then glanced up at me. It may have been my imagination, but I saw steam rising from his temples.

I smiled at him and rested my hand on the door handle. "Thank you for your time, Officer Farlow."

I hissed. "Clair!"

My persistent friend finally took that hint, calmly

stood and followed me. She called over her shoulder as we crossed the threshold. "Thanks Jimmy. So good to see you."

I'm pretty sure I heard him mutter. "It's Officer Farlow."

We were almost to the front door when Clair hailed another officer. "Hi, Joe. How are you?"

As he approached, I thought if I ever needed a policeman in Evelynton, this is the man I'd call. Slightly overweight, with a ready smile and kind eyes, I knew he would be helpful.

"Hey, Clair. What's up?"

She whispered. "I have a quick question for you." Glancing toward Officer Farlow's office, Clair grabbed Joe's arm and dragged him to a corner—out of Farlow's line of sight. "I won't keep you long. I think Jimmy wants me out of here."

Joe chuckled. "Nothing new there."

"Do you know anything about Eddy Garrison and Gary Edwards?"

"I remember them. I probably wouldn't but for the names. It was some years back. I hadn't been on the force very long when their info came across my desk. Couple of older guys that were suspected of petty theft. But they disappeared before we could bring them in for questioning. We never heard of them again. That was quite a while ago. Why do you ask?"

My friend gave a flirtatious lift of her shoulder. "No reason. I ran across their names."

Clair glanced toward the exit as if she was finished, but I knew better. "Oh, one more thing. What do you know about a woman named Joan who died of an overdose about ten years ago?"

"Can't remember anything like that. Do you have a last name?"

"It might have been Crandall."

"Sorry, I don't recall anyone by that name. You'd think I would with the manner of death. It's rare in Evelynton."

We heard a door opening somewhere in the hallway. Clair glanced that way and took a step back. "Thanks for the help. We better get going. Nice to see you."

On the sidewalk again, clouds had partially covered the afternoon sun, giving the town a sadly muted glow. Or it could have been my mood.

Clair glanced at me and shrugged. "I've exhausted my ideas, let's go home."

We returned to her car and drove out of Evelynton. As we merged onto the highway, I took a clean sheet of notebook paper to list my thoughts.

Joan Crandall died of a drug over-dose ten years earlier, but might have begun using soon after graduation. Or, did it begin while in high school?

Gary Edwards and Eddy Garrison, left town in the midst of a criminal inquiry, possibly to avoid questioning.

JF aka James Farlow got into trouble in school but went on to encourage his son to become a policeman.

B. Unknown person. People were unable or unwilling to identify him or her.

Peggy Clooney Larkin appeared older than her years. She seemed to be disturbed and hostile. Should I believe anything she said?

What did any of our discoveries have to do with my mother's experience in this town? My visit to Evelynton hadn't turned out the way I'd expected. Had I learned anything?

    I crumpled the paper and tossed it to the floor.

Chapter Fifteen

The drive home seemed endless, marked only by miles of soybean fields. With my head resting against the back of the seat, I could have fallen asleep but for a disturbing image. An image that kept reappearing in my thoughts no matter how often I banished it. That of one unhappy woman. The only person who'd ever uttered an unkind remark about my mother. That alone should tell me something. The woman was a liar.

Clair pulled the BMW into my driveway and parked close to the house. I'd unfastened my seat belt before she killed the engine. "Come on in. I owe you a dinner. I appreciate you taking the time to drive me to Evelynton."

"I'll take dinner. But you don't owe me anything. I loved seeing Rarity and Gloria. Jimmy Farlow, too. It's nice to know that some people never change."

I couldn't hold back the smirk and did my best imitation. "It's Officer Farlow, if you don't mind."

Clair laughed. "That never gets old."

She stood beside me on the porch while I searched for my house key. Once I'd pulled it from the depths of my handbag, I realized the effort had been unnecessary. "Shoot. The door's not even locked."

Clair shrugged. "It's a good thing we're in Twin

Fawn. And at least you remembered to leave the porch light on, this time."

She tagged along as I moved through the foyer to reach the living room light switch. "Now that you've spent a few hours in your mom's hometown, what did you think of it?"

"Peaceful on the whole. The Rare Curl was quaint. Sort of like stepping back in time. There are some lovely residents, but at least one who is not so friendly."

"Yep. There are miserable people in every town, but I don't believe Peggy's stories had anything to do with your mother."

On her way to the sofa to drop off her jacket, Clair stepped close to the window and peered out.

"What's so interesting out there? Is your car alright?"

"The car's fine. But there's someone out on the sidewalk. Some guy was staring at your house, but he's walked on, now."

I closed in beside Clair. "I don't see anyone. What did he look like?"

"Sort of big, I guess. But it was too dark to say for sure."

"It's probably one of my neighbors out for a walk. I'm sure you don't get that much out where you live." I dropped my handbag on the couch and headed for the kitchen. "How about chili for dinner? I made a pot yesterday. It's always good reheated."

The window steamed up as Clair continued to scan the street. "We don't have any close neighbors out in the country. It's a rare sight to see anyone walking after dark." She straightened and turned toward me. "Chili sounds great. Do you have crackers?"

I stood at the open refrigerator with my mind on other

things.

"Earth to Lib. Do you have crackers?"

"Um. Yes. They're in the pantry next to the oatmeal." I moved closer to the refrigerator and studied each shelf. "I just can't find the chili. It was right here." I laid my hand on the empty shelf as if I might touch the missing bowl that tended to be invisible.

Clair came up and peeked over my shoulder. "Not there now. Maybe you finished it and forgot."

I shut the refrigerator door and shook my head. "I did not eat a whole pot of chili. Besides, it was in the big red bowl my mother gave me." I checked the sink and the cupboard with no luck. "I love that bowl."

My encouraging friend grinned at me. "Don't worry about it. You're tired." She returned to the pantry. "I saw a can of chili in here. Let's have that."

I managed to catch the can as she tossed it to me. "I've lost my mind."

"No, you haven't. It's been a long day, and the trip to Evelynton proved more stressful than either of us expected."

I grabbed a pan and poured in the store-bought chili. While it was heating, I went to the pantry. "I have cookies for dessert."

"Great. What kind?"

I stood inside the pantry and shoved boxes from side to side on the shelves. Then, I leaned over to rummage through the trash container. "It looks like we won't have dessert after all. I can't find them. And don't tell me I probably ate them. The box is not in the garbage."

Clair came up behind me and put her arm around my shoulders. "Go into the living room and rest. I'll bring the chili and crackers. You'll feel better after dinner."

I gazed into the pantry one more time before turning to leave the kitchen. "Okay. But I did make chili yesterday. And I had cookies. Where are my cookies?"

She put up her hands. "I didn't take them." Softening her voice as if speaking to someone's elderly grandmother, she gave me a gentle push toward the living room. "Go sit down."

The canned chili was hot and filling. I remained quiet while we ate. Clair entertained herself with the television remote control until her cell phone diverted her attention.

"I just got the strangest text message. It's signed Peggy. The only Peggy I know is your mother's old friend—who wasn't really much of a friend."

"Really? Maybe she thought of something else. What did she have to say?"

"It's really for your mother."

"Tell me."

"She said to tell Kat that he knows where she lives, and he'll get her."

"He who? And what did she mean by *he will get her*?

Clair was tapping into her phone. "No clue. That's all it said. I'm texting her back."

Clair hit send and we stared at the screen, waiting for the answer. After an endless three minutes, we'd had no reward.

"I can't wait any longer. I'm calling her." Clair tapped her phone a few times, held it to her ear and then pulled it away. "It only rang once and went to voicemail. I'll leave a message."

Clair left the message requesting more information, and we waited again.

"Shoot. I wonder if she's blocked me."

"The woman's unhappy. She probably wanted to

cause trouble. She'd say anything to upset my mom."

Clair held the phone toward me. "Do you think I should give Katherine the message?"

"No. Delete it. I sure don't want to give my mother that ominous message. Besides, Mom doesn't know we've been prying into her past. How would I explain even knowing Peggy?"

"Right." She hit delete. "Done."

"I don't have much of an appetite after that. Are you finished?"

Clair handed me her bowl and spoon. "You wash. I'll dry." She had begun to follow me, but I soon found her staring out a window again. This time she stood at the window to the backyard.

"Libby, now there's someone prowling around out there." She pushed away from the window, marched to the back door and yanked it open. She shouted. "Who's out there? I see you. What are you doing?"

A familiar voice rang out from the shadows. "Sorry. It's me, Garrett Reed. My buddy lost his dog and I'm out here looking for it. Haven't seen a beagle wandering around, have you?"

Clair shouted. "Nope. Haven't seen it, but we'll let you know if we do."

"Thanks. I might have seen it go down the alley so I'm heading that way. Again, sorry to have disturbed you. Have a good night."

I attempted to reach the back door but Clair blocked my way. She whirled toward me with her hands on her hips. "What was he doing in your backyard?"

"I'm sure he was doing just what he said. Looking for a dog. Don't worry about it. It's Garrett." The simple knowledge that he was in the vicinity produced a warm fuzzy feeling in me.

Clair blew out a breath. "I guess you're right. I'm too suspicious."

I peeked around her, but saw no sign of Garrett. "I'll finish cleaning up. You go home and get some rest."

Clair picked up her jacket and bag and stood by the front door. "We had fun today. I'm not sure the trip accomplished anything other than adding to your mother's mystery, but now you've seen Evelynton. Thanks for supper."

I waved as she walked to her car. "Remember we're expected at the church tomorrow to organize the donated winter coats. I promised we'd be there right after work to get things started. The collection brought in tons of stuff. It all needs sorted for the guys to deliver to the homeless shelter in Indianapolis."

Yes, the mundane task of sorting winter coats. I looked forward to my life returning to normal. I wanted to forget about the unhappy woman in Evelynton as well as my mysteriously absent chili and cookies. Worrying about my mother's—probably non-existent—secret past had been exhausting. Even my stable friend, Clair, had become suspicious.

Chapter Sixteen

Clair held the door for Mom and me as we exited the church. "Who would have thought our little congregation could collect so many coats? When I saw the pile, I was afraid we'd be sorting all night, but it went fast. And the pizza the pastor ordered helped keep our spirits up."

My mother smiled. "The task is easy when friends work together."

Clair swiveled toward us. "Well ladies, this was fun. But I'm hosting an open house tomorrow, so I have some work to do before my day is finished. You two have a nice night." She waved as she took off across the parking lot.

I'd parked my Honda beside my mother's VW. While she climbed in her car, I decided I'd enjoyed her company and wasn't quite ready to give up on the day. "How about a movie at my house?"

"That would be perfect. I'll meet you there."

As soon as we got to the house, I popped in the DVD and prepared it to play. "Feel like popcorn tonight?"

My mother slid out of her shoes and sank into the corner of the sofa with her feet curled under her. "That sounds good. Did you lock the door?"

"Yes, I did. With the strange things going on, lately, I've become more conscious of security."

"I'm glad, dear. We can never be sure who might be roaming the streets, and I've had an uneasy feeling recently." She paused for a moment. "It's probably just old age.

I grinned at her. "It's a rare occasion that you admit to aging."

She flapped a hand at me. "Now, about the popcorn, let's have the homemade kind. Not the bagged stuff."

"Yes, Mother. The jar you brought the last time you were here is still in the pantry. I'll find it." I pulled out the popcorn and searched for my only sauce pan with a lid that fit.

"I'll help." She hopped off the sofa and walked barefoot to the kitchen. "You start heating the oil for the corn. I'll melt the butter."

She pulled open a cupboard and leaned inside "Where's that little pan? The one with the green enamel on the outside." Her voice echoed inside the cupboard.

"I don't know where that is. Is it the one you brought with the popcorn? I thought you took it home with you."

"Yes, that's the one, dear. I left it, thinking you would have more use for it than I would. It's the perfect size to melt butter." She got down on her knees and crawled deeper into the cupboard.

Pots and pans rattled from the cupboard while I rummaged in the pantry for the oil. A loud bang brought me out of the closet, expecting to see my mother injured. "Are you alright? Did you hit your head?"

Mother pulled out of the cupboard and sat on the floor looking up at me. "No, I didn't hit my head. I thought you dropped something."

"Nope, not me. Do you think it was something outside?"

We didn't stew about it for long. The answer came with a violent pounding on the front door. Mother pushed herself up from the floor. "What in the world?"

I took a few tentative steps toward the hallway and peeked around the corner. A constant pounding continued.

I stood staring at the door while building up the courage to answer it, but backed up when loud taunting words mingled with the racket. The man's voice sounded like rolling thunder. "Kat Baron! Open the door. Don't you want to welcome an old friend? It's Bernie. You haven't forgotten me, have you?"

I heard a gasp and turned to see my mother leaning against the counter with her hand covering her mouth.

I gaped at her. "He called you Kat Baron. Nobody calls you that…except." I decided not to finish that thought.

My attention returned to the door. "Come on little Kat, don't hide from me." The angry ranting continued. "I thought I'd have fun tormenting you for a while, but got bored with it. A little homecooked food was nice, but I deserve a lot more. You need to pay."

A steady pounding went on and grew louder as did the man's voice. "It's time you faced me. You ruined my life and it's time to pay up."

I turned to mother, clenching my fists to keep from trembling. "I think he's kicking the door. This is crazy. What are we going to do? Should we call the police?"

I looked to my mother for support, but her eyes were closed. She shook her head and breathed out, "I should have known. I felt a strong sense of dread when I saw him. Couldn't believe it was really him. He's changed so much."

"Who? Do you know this person?"

She hissed. "I know him."

Mother opened her eyes, and I watched her face transform. Muscles flexed, features hardened. Was I imagining things? She glared at the door like a mother bear guarding her cub.

"Mom."

She put up a hand to silence me. "We'll talk later. Right now, I have something to take care of."

She stretched up to her full height, all four feet, eleven inches. Her chest expanded as she filled her lungs. She pointed at me. "You stay here." Then, she stomped into the hallway and shouted. No, not a shout. It was more of a roar that erupted from my petite mother's throat. "Get away from here, Bernie. I'm warning you. I'll call the police. You don't want to meet up with them again."

"Bernie? You know that guy? Who is he?"

The relentless pummeling of the door accelerated. Pain shot behind my eyes. I shouted to my mother. "The door isn't strong enough. He's going to come crashing through." I scanned the kitchen counter. "Where's my phone?" I checked my jeans pockets. No phone. "I left it in the living room. Do you have yours?"

She shook her head. "No. Mine's in my purse. You run in there and call the police. I'll guard the door." Mother stood with her legs apart and arms up as if she were a prize fighter. "Lord, give me the strength."

"What do you mean you'll guard the door? Whoever is out there is violent and sounds really big."

She turned her glare at me and pointed toward the

living room. "Go!"

"Okay." I grabbed a sauce pan for protection, scooted past the vibrating door frame and plunged into the living room in search of a phone.

Glancing over my shoulder I saw my mother edge close to the door. Much too close to the danger. "Mom, get away from there before he comes through. It sounds like he's kicking it." The wooden door had serviced the house for my entire life, but the old wood wouldn't take much more abuse. I should have had it replaced, but I'd never expected a need to defend myself.

I snatched my cellphone from the coffee table and fumbled with the simple three-digit emergency number. As calmly as I could manage, I reported the problem, then prayed the police would arrive before the maniac forced his way in.

For my mother's sake I knew I had to stay calm. At her age, how much could she take? I gripped the sauce pan and ran past the front door to get back into the kitchen. The room was empty. "Mom?"

Mom said she'd be guarding the door, but must have listened to me when I told her to stay away from it. Where was she? Maybe in the pantry? I opened the door and peeked in. She wasn't there.

The pounding seemed to be getting louder. I glanced at the door and saw a crack had appeared around the latch. We didn't have much time.

The next thing I heard confused me. More banging, but it was from the back of the house. Were there two of them? Were they breaking in from both sides? I slapped my hand over my mouth to keep from screaming.

Random thoughts coursed through my brain. A gang of criminals had gotten the wrong address. No, that couldn't be it. The one in front called my mother by name, so it was someone acquainted with her.

Who would be mad at a librarian? How angry could you get about fines from an overdue library book?

Wielding my saucepan, I shouted above the noise, "Mom, where are you? There's someone trying to get in the back, now. Are you hiding?"

I frantically followed the noise at the back of the house, waving my sauce pan above my head and praying I wouldn't find someone coming through a window. But the racket came from the bathroom. That window was much too small for anyone to crawl through, so it would hold them off.

I found my poor mother there in the bathroom. She'd become hysterical. The linen closet door stood open. She had yanked out the shelves and thrown them on the floor. The woman was kicking the back wall of the closet.

"What are you doing? We can't hide in there. It's too small." She kept kicking until the boards loosened and popped out revealing an open area. A secret hiding place? "Mother, that's no good. It's still much too small for us to get in."

My mother ignored my pleading, reached in and pulled out a parcel wrapped in newspaper. After she dropped the paper to the floor, I saw a gun in her hand. It seemed to me that she was moving in slow motion as she reached back into the secret compartment and pulled out a box. It contained ammunition.

I stood in stunned silence while she loaded the handgun with the precision of the detectives I watched on television. How did she know how to do that?

"Mother. I don't know where that came from, but I don't think you should be messing with it. It might go off. Let's hide. The police will be here soon."

The woman brushed past me on her way to the hallway. "Don't be silly, Liberty. Where do you think it came from? I put it there. Now, get behind me! Not too close." I'd never heard her use that tone of voice. It got my attention, and I did as I was told.

Holding the revolver in two hands she stalked toward the still rattling and splintering front door. Then I heard an explosion. When I opened my eyes, because I guessed I'd closed them, I saw a hole in the bottom of the door.

There's no accounting for the strange thoughts that go through your mind in a crisis. I worried about how mad my mother would be about the damage, once she'd regained her senses.

Everything became still. The pounding and shouting from outside had ceased. Then my mother yelled. "Are you still out there, Bernie? Get away from here. I promise, if you come through that door, I'll shoot to kill. I'll put a hole right through your heart. You know I can."

I was shaking so hard I could barely breathe. Thoughts floated around in my head. The words "*a hole right through you heart"* surfaced. Had she heard that on some television program? My mother would never hurt anyone.

"Mother, how did you know how to shoot? You told me you hated guns."

My mother calmly maintained her vigil guarding the door. "That was the truth. I do hate guns. But Liberty, one must recognize their usefulness."

A distant whine sounded and grew louder. Sirens approached. I slumped against the wall and took a deep breath while making an effort to sort out my thoughts.

With the threat seemingly gone, I continued to

process the events. "Wait." I spun toward the bathroom. "How long has that secret compartment been there? How did you know you would find the gun?" I cocked my head. "And the bullets."

My mother glanced at me. "Liberty dear, I lived here long before you did."

My brain was spinning. Who was this woman? Where was my sweet, mild-mannered mama?"

The squad car screeched to a halt at the curb. Car doors slammed, footsteps approached, and a policeman announced himself. Mother lowered the gun. "Is that you Arnie?" I felt safe with Arnie on the scene. He'd served as the Twin Fawn police chief for nearly twenty years. I couldn't remember anyone else in the job, and in my mind, he hadn't changed in those years. I guess he'd gained a few pounds—more than a few. And lost some hair. Still, he struck an imposing figure in his uniform.

"It's me Mrs. Cassell. There's nobody out here. We're checking all around the house. You're safe now. Open the door."

"Okay. I'm so glad you're here. Just a minute."

I reached for the bolt lock, still fastened but no longer flush with the door frame. Mom grabbed my wrist. "Wait." At that, she ran to the living room and slid the gun under a sofa cushion, returned and calmly pulled open the door. She took the lead in filling the officer in on the events. I noticed she omitted her part in the shooting.

I would have talked to the officer. Except my mind had begun swirling again, and I couldn't get the words to come out in the correct order. I was still wondering what had happened, and how, and why. Not where. I had a grip on that question. There had been a gun fight in my foyer.

Arnie took notes as my mother rattled off the facts. The officer may not have been the brightest small-town cop, but it didn't take him long to notice there might have been more going on than Mom had reported. He pointed to the bullet hole in my door and looked at me. "Do you own a firearm?"

I gave him a glassy-eyed head shake. Fortunately, my mother had her wits about her. "Sorry, Arnie. Of course, you would notice the door was damaged from the inside. And it's obviously a bullet hole. I must be losing it." She returned to the couch and pulled out her handgun.

Arnie focused on me again. "I trust you have a permit for this, Miss Cassell?" I knew I was in trouble because Arnie had never called me Miss Cassell. Ever.

I opened my mouth and closed it. I shrugged, and finally managed, "A permit? I didn't even know there was a gun in the house."

He seemed a little doubtful, but turned his attention to my mother who said, "She's telling the truth. It's mine. And yes, I have a permit."

I left Arnie and my mother to sort out the details and wandered into the bathroom to take a look at my linen closet. My bath towels still lay strewn across the floor. The shelves Mom had pulled out lay on top of the towels. Over those, lay the boards she had removed from the back wall of the closet, and crinkled newspaper lay scattered across the floor.

I stared at the secret compartment, now empty. How long had it been there? I grew up in this house. There was not a corner, space, or hiding place my brother and I hadn't discovered. Or so I thought.

Why didn't I know my mother could shoot a gun? How could I have missed that she owned one? Did my father know?

When I returned to the hallway, Arnie had confiscated the handgun and stood inspecting it. "Vintage Smith and Wesson. Nice weapon, Mrs. Cassell. I'll have to take this with me. But I'll take good care of it. I'll give you a receipt and make sure you get it back."

To my surprise, and relief, I found I could think and talk at the same time. "You can't do that, Arnie. You're leaving us defenseless. What would we do if that madman showed up again?"

"Don't worry, I think he's gone for good, but I'll have someone circling the neighborhood all night. They will make a pass by your house about every twenty minutes. I'd advise that you spend the night somewhere else until you get the door repaired. You'll sleep better." Arnie turned to leave.

My mother, always polite, thanked him and waved goodbye from the porch. When the squad car left the curb, she pointed toward my room. "Get your things. You'll come stay with me in my apartment tonight. It isn't safe here. That door won't keep anyone out, and I don't trust the Twin Fawn police to protect you. They haven't had any practice. Nothing ever happens here."

"Okay." I began the trek to my room but stopped.

"Wait. Who was that man?" After a pause, I demanded, "Why was there a gun in the bathroom? Where did it come from?"

Mother had stepped into the kitchen and collected my loaf of bread and carton of milk. She noticed me watching her. "I'm almost out at my place." She shooed me with her hand and pointed toward my bedroom, again. "And as for your questions, they can wait. I don't want to talk about it now. I'll tell you everything when we get to my place. Pack your bag."

~~

My mother drove in silence. Her attention darting between the road ahead and the rearview mirror. My mind was whirling. Each time I asked a question she simply shook her head.

By the end of the trip my heart rate had returned to somewhat normal. I dropped my bag in the middle of Mom's living room. "Start talking, because I'm thinking I might be in the middle of a nightmare and can't get out of it."

My aggravating mother sounded calm and cool. "Yes, dear. First, I want to get out of these clothes." She turned and walked to her bedroom. I sighed and picked up my suitcase. "I guess I'll change, too."

After stowing my things in the spare room, I put on sweatpants and a t-shirt and wandered back to the living room to wait for her. When she returned, she wore pink pajamas and matching robe with fluffy slippers.

"Tell me what's going on."

"Just a minute." She walked to the hall closet and reached under a stack of bed sheets. I was afraid to guess what might appear from there.

"Oh, crap. Is that another one?"

"Yes, a Smith and Wesson Revolver. Also, in great condition. Identical to the one I gave Arnie."

"Of course, it is. So, do you have an arsenal?" I wanted to be kidding, but was learning far too much about this woman to rely on it.

"No dear, just the two. I didn't think I'd need any more than that. In the last few years, I'd even considered getting rid of these. But it's such a hassle. If I wanted to sell them, I would have to be sure the buyer wasn't prohibited from owning a firearm. Then, how would I advertise it for sale? Can you imagine trying to sell a gun in Twin Fawn? The stories that would circulate? I didn't want to deal with a bunch of nosy neighbors."

She sat in the rocking chair with the weapon in her lap. It was the same chair that had rocked my nephews as babies. "Bernie tracked me to the house and obviously thought I still lived there. He might just as easily find me here, so let me load this. Then we'll go to the kitchen and have a nice cup of tea."

I watched as she held the firearm in her left hand, popped out the cylinder and, with her right hand, quickly slid in five bullets. I counted. She clicked the cylinder back into place as if it was something she'd done a thousand times. Maybe she had.

Flashing her sweet grandma smile. "There, all done. Let's get that tea."

She padded into the kitchen. I followed, still wondering who this woman might be, and why she seemed so comfortable with that weapon.

Did I really want to know?

Chapter Seventeen

I cowered in the corner staring at my mother's kitchen counter. Shiny, perfectly clean, pristine. Pale yellow crocks lined up holding sugar, salt, and flour. And the big one on the end. Anyone who knew her would reach for that one. She kept it filled with cookies. A welcome gift to children, grandchildren, friends and strangers. I fought the urge to lift the lid and see what treats it might contain today.

Above the sink hung a framed landscape of green fields and quiet stream. The one thing my mother had missed after moving into her apartment was watching the sunset while washing dinner dishes. That print echoed the peace and serenity every daughter should expect in her mother's kitchen. I stood in the sweet, comfy room where my mother had so often served me lunch over the past few months.

Tonight, one ugly stain blemished this special place. The intimidating black handgun resting on the counter near the stove. Ominous, frightening. My brain kept directing my attention to it again and again, as if the weapon would soon disappear, because it didn't belong in this dimension of the universe. How could it? Being so at odds with my mother, with her life, and my life. The awareness that the truth of her existence was not what I'd been so sure of slowly pushed its way to the surface of my reality.

I lowered myself into the chair across from my mother at a table covered with pale blue cloth printed with red and yellow flowers. The pattern had always seemed so like my mother. Now I wondered. Was it some sort of camouflage? I couldn't help scanning the room for missed signals of this alternate personality.

I flinched when the tea kettle shot out a whistle from the stove. My mother calmly got up and poured the boiling water into the teapot, and placed cups on the table.

Settled back into her chair, she took a deep breath and gave me a sad smile. "I know you're confused about this. I'm sorry I failed to prepare you. The possibility of the past revisiting me, well, it was inevitable."

I clutched my empty cup. "Tell me what's going on. Who was that madman? Did you call him Bernie? You said he tracked you. From where? And why would he follow you?"

She nodded. "Yes, you have a right to those questions. I should have told you long ago. I guess I thought this would never happen." Her voice was soft. The same peaceful quality that had soothed me so often in my life, convincing me that I was safe. There was no monster under the bed. None in the closet. All was well.

The story she was about to tell would change everything I believed about my mother. Her tale shook my world and took my breath away.

I'd been wrong. There *was* a monster under the bed.

My mother reached across the pale blue tablecloth to hold my hand. "The man making all that racket, and trying to beat down the front door, was someone from my past. His name is Bernard Quinn. I knew him when I was in high school. He'd had a hard life and was probably the most dangerous of my friends. Back then, I found the trait attractive, even exciting." A slight smile crossed her face.

"Was he in your class in high school?"

"No. Bernie was older and out of school, but he hung around with me and a few of my school friends."

"That was so long ago. Why is he here, now?"

"The last time I saw him was just before he was sent to prison. Time doesn't always heal wounds. I'm afraid his time behind bars didn't do him any good."

"Prison? I can't imagine you were friends with anyone like that. You've always cautioned me about hanging out with the wrong people. Isn't there something in Proverbs about 'don't make friends with a wrathful man lest you become entangled in his web'?"

Mom smiled and pointed an index finger at me. "Very good. You were listening after all." She gave my hand a pat. "Where do you think I learned the seriousness of that verse?"

"The tea is ready." She picked up the teapot and carefully filled our cups.

Shifting her gaze back to me, "I can see I need to start at the beginning."

Mother blew into her cup to cool the tea. "Bernie wasn't such a bad kid, although you're right. I shouldn't have been hanging around with him. He used to have a crush on me and I'm afraid I took advantage of that friendship. Maybe he shouldn't have been associating with me."

"You're confusing me."

Shrugging, she continued. "I was sixteen, and he must have been about nineteen. There was a group of us who spent a lot of time together. It was Bernie, Peggy Clooney, James, and me." She tipped her head to the side. "Oh yes. then there was Gary and Eddy. I don't recall their last names. And Joan, I think. I can't remember much about her. I've spent years trying to put all of this out of my mind."

A tear glistened in the corner of her eye. She dabbed at it with a tissue and continued. "You'd probably call us a gang, because we were fairly defiant of authority. In reality, we were bored kids with too much time on our hands. And too much imagination for our own good.

"The bunch of us came up with a stupid scheme to break the law." She shook her head. "Who am I kidding? It was my scheme. I was the youngest, yet always the leader. Whatever wild plan I came up with, they followed. And of course, Bernie had that crush." She tipped her head back and seemed to be looking into the past. "He wasn't bad looking back then. I liked him, but I had no emotional attachment. I was in it for the adventure. We all were. Or so I thought."

I stared into my cup, not wanting to meet my mother's eyes. I had a dreadful feeling that I really didn't want to hear her story.

She clutched her cup in both hands as she spoke. "You're aware I grew up in Evelynton, Indiana. It was a small town, then. Smaller even than Twin Fawn. That made our games all the more exciting because we knew the police officers personally. Some of them coached softball. Or they were friends with our folks. We saw them around town every day." She laughed. "We were so arrogant. We strutted around as if we owned the town."

"Arrogant? No. You are the humblest person I know."

She raised her eyebrows at me and continued. "Our great mission was to rob as many stores as we could, but only the small businesses. Gary, Ed, and Peggy weren't thrilled about it at first. They were afraid we'd get caught. But I could be convincing. I reasoned that if we only stole a small amount of cash from each store, the police wouldn't consider it worth their time, and probably wouldn't even look for us. It took a while, but I swayed the whole gang to my way of thinking.

"After that, it became a game. We spent time learning the trade. Did you know I can pick a lock? Or I could back then. We became adept at opening doors and prying open windows. I loved the feeling of getting into places I shouldn't go. I was careful in choosing a target. Most places didn't spend much on security. Why would they? In such a little burg?"

Mother saw the horror reflected on my face and reached out to hold my hand. "I didn't want to hurt anyone. None of us did. We figured we weren't causing anyone harm. We didn't understand that the thefts hurt the store owners. And in the end, my friends suffered the consequences. They spent time in jail. Everyone labeled them as bad kids. Their involvement crushed their families. Their futures ruined. They had to repay everything we stole."

"They? But not you?"

"No, not me."

She rested her elbows on the table and sipped her tea. "You see, Liberty, what I didn't know at the time was that right always wins. Sin catches up with you and demands payment."

Mom shut her eyes for a moment, then began again. "I remember the night it caught up with us. Bernie managed to open the door to White's Drug Store. We walked right in laughing and acting like it was our little playground. There was a coffee counter at the back of the store, and I hopped up on one of the stools. I sat there spinning around like the child I was. Gary and Eddy found boxes of soda pop and helped themselves to a couple of bottles. Bernie, Peggy and James were at the cash register. Joan was hanging around somewhere. She was always the quiet one."

A shadow passed over my mother's face. Her voice dropped to a whisper. "I remember it like it was yesterday."

Her hands trembled as she paused to drink her tea before continuing. "The police were smarter than we gave them credit for. They were waiting for us. We hadn't been inside for more than five minutes when the front door burst open. They came storming in, shouting and aiming guns at us."

With closed eyes, she dipped her head. "I'll never forget the sounds. Men were yelling for us to hit the floor. Peggy and Joan were screaming."

Mother ran her hands through her hair and turned her attention back to me. "It wasn't a game anymore. I was scared to death. Most of my friends did get on the floor. Bernie came running, pulled me off of that stool, and pushed me toward the back door. I got through, but he didn't make it. I don't know if they caught him inside the store or maybe they were waiting outside as well. All I know is, I ran. And I didn't look back. Down the street and through every dark alley I could find. Didn't even pay attention to where I was going. I just kept running until I felt so sick that I couldn't take another step. When I took time to look around, I found myself outside of town in the country somewhere."

My heart raced. Dizziness caused the room to sway. I wanted her to stop talking, but had no choice but to listen to the whole story. This revelation changed everything I knew about my life.

Running her hand across her face to swipe away tears that had made their way down her pale cheek, she continued. "I remember shaking so hard I couldn't keep my teeth from chattering. I knew the police would catch up with me. I kept searching for the headlights of squad cars, and thinking if they were on foot, there would be flashlights. But they didn't come. After a while I walked back into town and sneaked into my house. I got cleaned up and went to bed. The next morning, I told my mother I had a headache, and stayed home from school. I lay on the couch all day waiting for the authorities to come pounding on the door."

Tea splashed from my cup because my hands were trembling, waiting, with her, for the knock on the door.

Mom raised her shoulders in a shrug and flashed a slight smile. "They never came."

She slumped into her chair and sipped her tea. "The next day I went back to class and pretended nothing had happened. By that time, I thought maybe I'd dreamed the whole thing."

For a moment, I almost smiled thinking my mother was going to laugh and say, "And it was a dream!" I hoped she would. I wanted her to. But there was no explaining away the madman at the house or the handgun on the counter.

Mom continued. "You can imagine there was quite a stir at school. All our gang, all my friends had been caught that night and put in jail. Everyone but me. In the end the five who were my age, Peggy, Joan, Gary, James and Eddy got a few months of probation and community service. But Bernie was older and had been in trouble before. They blamed it on him and said he was the instigator who had corrupted the others. He went to prison."

Tears filled my mother's eyes. "In all the proceedings, no one turned me in."

She picked up the teapot and refilled her cup. "I never spoke to any of them again. Of course, Bernie was gone. None of the others got back into regular classes until just before graduation, and I pretended I didn't know them."

"You see, I'd come up with another plan. I recreated myself into the perfect student and perfect daughter. Your grandmother was shocked when I volunteered to wash the dinner dishes every day. I cleaned my room without being asked. I studied. If I wasn't in school, I was in my room doing homework. That's why I finished school with such excellent grades."

"Didn't anyone suspect? Someone must have known you were part of the group. The gang."

"If they did, they didn't mention it to me. I put the past out of my mind and refused to even think about what we did. What I did."

"What about Grandma and Grandpa?"

"They had never paid much attention to who I hung around with, so they had no idea I was involved. I know they heard about the crime spree and probably thought 'Those poor people. What did they do wrong to have raised criminals?' Little did they know I'd caused it all."

My mother smiled at me and seemed to recall a pleasant time. "I left town right after graduation, found a little community college in Warrenton and took a two-year course. So, I made my father happy and had learned a trade. I never went back to Evelynton."

She sobered again. "But there was never a moment that I didn't expect the police to be at my door. That is, until I got married. Then with the name change, and the move to Twin Fawn, I felt I was free of it all. All links severed."

"What about the box I found in the attic? Why didn't you want me to see it?"

"Oh, the one link to my past that for some stupid reason, I kept. It wasn't the yearbooks I worried about. I'd stashed some silly costume jewelry from one of the stores I'd robbed. Not worth much, but my parents had never let me wear jewelry, so I kept it as a symbol of my independence." Mother shook her head. "I never wore it. Just knowing I had it was enough. Not a very smart move. I kept the one thing that could link me to the thefts. But over the years I'd forgotten it. When you told me you found that box, I panicked. How would I have explained it?"

I decided not to tell her how Clair and I had found jewelry and tucked it back in the bottom of the box. I leaned back in my chair, my thoughts whirling. Grateful for a moment of quiet.

My mother leaned toward me. "Did you ever wonder why your grandparents always came here to visit, but we never went to see them in Evelynton? Oh, I know you did. You asked me."

I shook my head. "I guess I thought that's the way

everyone did things."

"It's the way I wanted it. I couldn't stomach the thought of seeing the stores I'd robbed, or the possibility of running into any of my old friends."

I pictured my grandparents. "There was a time I wondered why Grandma and Grandpa never invited us to visit. It was when one of my friends went to visit their grandparents."

"They invited us once. Just one time. When I declined, they never brought it up again."

"They came here to see us. Every Christmas, Easter, Thanksgiving, my birthdays."

"Yes, they were happy to drive to see us. They never said anything, and I didn't think about it until after they were gone, but I suspect they always knew the truth. They probably connected me with a few of the kids who were caught and knew me well enough to guess I'd been involved that night."

She shook her head and gave a sad smile. "I bet they were scared to death to bring it up for fear I'd confess. Then, being the good people they were, they would have taken me straight to the police. But as it was, they could ignore the possibility their little girl was a thief. I was still their innocent princess. Their pride and joy."

Mom paused and took the time to finish her tea. "So, about Bernie, the man who tried to break in. He was the oldest of our group, and as I said, had been in some trouble before. Nothing serious. But he got the hardest sentence because of it. Later, if I thought about him at all, I figured he didn't turn me in because he wanted to protect me. He was in love."

She put her hand on my wrist. "The crush he had on me, the feelings he had for me made him vulnerable.

Men don't like to feel vulnerable or taken advantage of. Anger must have been building in him all this time. I suspect the emotions turned to hate. I'm sorry you had to experience the unleashing of that pent up fury."

Mom breathed out a sigh. "I'm so sorry about your house. We'll have to call a repairman tomorrow."

"It's alright. The house can be repaired. I'm glad he didn't catch you alone." I pointed to the handgun on the counter. "Although it seems you can take care of yourself."

She nodded. "I can."

Mom shrugged and rolled her eyes. "To continue the story, I moved to Twin Fawn without knowing anyone here. I didn't want to. That was part of recreating myself. A new life. No past. But I discovered I was lonely. Being a new person on my own wasn't all that fun. When I met your father, I sort of flung myself into his arms and never let go. He didn't seem to mind that I never talked about my past. We wanted to live in the moment, and he loved me just as I was. We got married two months later." She cracked a smile and gave a little giggle. "Maybe he knows all about me now. I'll have to face him someday, and he may want to talk to me about my escapades."

"You had to keep some hard secrets. I'm pretty sure Dad will be forgiving. But what are we going to do about that Bernie guy? He's violent and is still out there walking free. Why didn't you tell the police his name?"

"I know I should have. But I want to talk to him. I turned my life around and need to help him do the same. He might not even have been involved if not for his feelings for me. He served time, paid for his crime. I got off scot-free. I don't know how long he's been on my trail, but he's finally caught up with me and I need to face him. I hope he will be calm enough to listen. I hope he can forgive me."

I shook my head and took a sip of tea, now barely warm. "I don't believe it. You're telling me a story about someone who just isn't you. Please tell me this is some kind of elaborate joke. Are you trying to warn me away from Garrett? I'm a little old for that. You should have told me this story when I was in middle school."

She squinted at me. "About Garrett. There is something about him that is unsettling." She waved a hand. "We'll talk about that another time. But you're right, I was a different person when I lived in Evelynton. By the time I married your father and you were born, I'd changed. I was guilty then. Still am, but I'm discovering I can be forgiven." Those thoughts brought a sweet smile to her face.

She clenched her jaw causing her expression to harden. "Though there may still be consequences."

I scrubbed my fingers across my scalp to release tension. "I can't wrap my head around this. How could you have kept such a secret all these years? I always thought you told me everything."

"I told you everything except what I thought might hurt you. And I shoved everything else to the back of my mind. Pretending long enough causes the bad stuff to disappear."

A smile snaked across her face. "I think I was right in protecting you. See what a fine woman you've become. You have a good life."

"Except for the madman at the door."

"Yes, except for that."

"Knowing you and how you feel about truth and honesty, I still don't know how you kept such a secret."

"I was determined. I thought if I was a really good person, I could make up for the crimes I'd committed." She rolled her eyes. "I discovered it takes more than that."

She shrugged as she jiggled the teapot, checking the contents. "My life was fine on the outside. But internally, I've never been free of the guilt of my crimes. Recently, I've been working to fix that. Pastor Tom and Julie Prescott have been helping me with some counseling. I'm coming to terms with what I did and figuring out how to make amends."

I couldn't help but laugh. "That's why you've been spending so much time at the church at night! You better let Chad in on the secret. He's been worried you were up to something with the pastor."

She raised her eyebrows. "Oh dear. He's another one who deserves the whole truth. I put it off too long with you. I'd prefer he found out without anyone trying to crash through his door."

I shook my head, trying to clear it. "I still can't put it all together."

My mother stood and picked up her cup. "Let's go somewhere more comfortable and I'll see if I can fill in the gaps."

I watched, still unbelieving, as she retrieved the handgun from the counter and slipped it into the pocket of her pink robe. Following her to the living room, I pinched myself, hoping I would soon wake up from this nightmare.

Chapter Eighteen

Mom returned to her rocking chair causing it to sway slowly with a familiar, somehow comforting creak. Her new cozy gray sofa drew me in. I settled into it and grabbed a designer-suggested cream-colored throw pillow to hold against my chest. Lilies filled a vase on the end table. A petal from one of the blossoms had fallen and I wanted to retrieve it, but found I didn't have the energy.

As in the kitchen, the atmosphere in her living room reflected the sweet, gentle woman who had raised me. But who *had* raised me? Had I ever really known her? "Mom, when are you going to tell the police what you know? Arnie treated it as a random break-in, but you knew who it was and probably what's behind his madness."

She closed her eyes for a moment while drawing a deep breath. "Now Liberty, what could I tell them? I didn't see his face. I only heard his voice. And it's been so many years. Maybe I'm mistaken. It could have been someone else."

I narrowed my eyes at her. "He called you by name and told you his."

"Oh yes. There is that." She raised her shoulders.

"You're right. It's time I faced up to the truth. I've been running away from it, but deep down I knew I hadn't escaped."

She put a hand on her forehead. "Once I tell the story to the police, you know everyone in Twin Fawn will be talking about it. There are no secrets in a small town."

"People love you. They know what a good person you are now. They'll have to face the fact that you haven't always been perfect. So what? Everyone has something in their past they're ashamed of."

She shook her head and closed her eyes for a moment. "Not everyone has quite this much on their conscience."

That almost stopped me. I had to agree with her. But I pushed on. This woman had spent her life helping me navigate life's trials. It was my turn to encourage my mother. "They will understand that all this happened when you were a child."

"Thank you, dear. Of course, you're right. The truth must come out. And, truly, I've grown tired of being the superwoman my friends have come to expect."

She leaned back in her chair, setting it rocking. "Chad will need to be warned of what's coming, so I'll call him first thing in the morning. Then I'll contact the police."

She let her head rest against the back of the chair. "I'm too tired to even think right now. Let's get some sleep."

Mother unfolded her tiny body from the chair and switched off the lamp. "Leave your cup. We'll get it in the morning."

She slumped as she walked to her bedroom. I'd never seen the woman look so defeated. The sluggishness of my own legs surprised me as I made my way to the guest room. I'd barely hit the pillow before sinking into deep sleep.

~~

Rumbles of thunder. Running. Growling? Momma chasing after me, laughing. Claps of thunder. Is it going to rain? More thunder. Louder. I fought my way from the depths of the dream and struggled to open my eyes. Thunder roared in the distance.

But as I listened, I knew it was not thunder. Reality surfaced with the racket of fists beating on the apartment door. I shook myself awake and untangled my legs from the blankets.

When I'd rolled off the bed and stumbled to the hallway, I found my mother standing in the doorway of her room. As our eyes met, she lowered the cell phone from her ear. "He's found me quicker than I imagined. I've called the police. Someone should be here any minute." She tucked the phone into the pocket of her robe. Her other hand held the Smith and Wesson.

The pommeling continued and my temples began to throb in rhythm. Not thinking clearly, I turned to go to the front door. "This has got to stop."

"Liberty! Stay away from there." Mother's voice pierced the air, bringing me to a halt. I backed up and clung to the hallway wall.

"He might break through. What if he has a gun? If he shoots through the door, you don't want to be in front of it." I fought to understand the commands my mother shouted. "Get back in your room and lock the door. Push the chest in front of it."

Between the pain in my head and revelations of the evening, I lost patience. I shouted back. "I'm not hiding while you're out here dealing with that maniac."

"Don't argue with me, Liberty Breeze. He's after me, not you. I can protect myself. But I don't want you to get caught in the crossfire."

Disobeying my mother again, I ran past her to the kitchen. Once there, I found her cast iron skillet. Heavy enough to knock a man out. Might even stop a bullet. "I'm not hiding. I can fight."

"For goodness sakes, child. Go to your room."

I shouted over the noise. "Really Mother? I'm a grown woman."

She blew out a breath and stared at me. "Alright, but stay out of range in case he's armed."

The rough, gravelly voice thundered from behind the door. "You won't get away from me again, Kat Baron. You ran off while I served my time, paid for my crime. I even paid for *your* crime. Did you ever come to see me? Did you ever even write?"

The man's voice lowered a notch. "Do you know how hard it is to find a job when you've spent time in the joint? Employers wouldn't even talk to me. I spent years cleaning up other people's garbage."

I allowed myself a moment of pity. But the roaring returned. "You ruined my life!" The only barricade between my mother and a madman shook with the force of his body crashing into it.

I pressed my back against the wall and held up the skillet, ready for an attack. "How much longer will the door hold?"

My mother shouted. "Bernie, stop. Please understand that I'm sorry for all of this. Let me explain."

The pounding ceased, though it still echoed in my ears.

She moved closer to danger and spoke through the door. "I'm so sorry. I didn't mean for you to take the brunt of the punishment. I was young and stupid. And so scared. I had no experience in dealing with the police, so I pretended not to know anything. I couldn't tell my parents. By the time I heard you went to prison, I'd pushed the whole ordeal so far out of my mind, I actually believed that I'd had no part in it."

The man's gruff, angry laugh rumbled from behind the door. "What kind of excuse is that? Poor little scared girl. Afraid to tell her momma." He laughed again, this time verging on hysterical. "Grow up and face the consequence."

There were tears in my mother's eyes. "I will, Bernie. I'll go to the authorities and confess my part in the crimes."

"Too late for that. You didn't show up for us then, but you will face me, now."

Sirens sounded in the distance, growing louder as our rescuers approached.

Even as I breathed a sigh of relief, the crashing resumed with more urgency. Banging and battering. I envisioned the monster bursting through before help arrived.

Suddenly it stopped. The racket had ceased. It seemed an unearthly silence enveloped the building, until police officers shouted commands broke the spell. "Get face down on the floor. Put your hands behind your back."

A few minutes later, we heard Arnie's familiar voice. "It's okay Mrs. Cassell. We've got him. He's handcuffed and won't be causing you anymore trouble, tonight."

My mother approached the door and carefully

released the deadbolt. She opened the door a few inches to peak through before pulling it wide.

I stood beside my mother in the doorway and saw the officer's gaze rest on the Smith & Wesson for an instant before flicking away. Mother slid the gun behind her back.

Two officers lifted Bernie to his feet and dragged him out of the building. All I saw of the madman was shaggy gray hair and big scuffed work-boots, but I knew I'd seen him before. He'd been in the hardware store, and I'd tripped over him at church.

Between the two officers, he had almost reached the squad car waiting at the curb when my mother whispered. "I'm sorry, Bernie."

Strength left my legs. I reached for the wall and slid down to the floor.

Arnie glanced at me. "Are you alright Libby?"

I managed a polite smile. "Yes, thank you. I'm okay. I'm just fine."

From the floor, I watched Arnie take notes as my mother told her story—a short version.

With the monster in custody, I should have been relieved.

But what trouble still awaited our family?

Chapter Nineteen

The autumn breeze cooled my over-heated cheeks as we stood outside. Two squad cars started their engines and pulled from the curb. Turning back to Mom's apartment I caught sight of a near-by neighbor peeking through his slightly open door, but he slammed it shut as soon as we made eye contact. My mother gave me a crooked smile and whispered. "It's a good thing most of the residents are deaf. They can't hear a thing once they remove their hearing aids for the night."

Later, when I crawled into bed, the clock read two thirty-five. I worked my way through a list of mental exercises and breathing tricks in an effort to quiet the turmoil in my head. But sleep wouldn't come. Instead, events of the evening replayed in my mind. I tossed and turned wondering what I could have done differently. Sometime in the night I saw a light under my bedroom door and got up to check.

My mother carried a glass to her room. "I'm sorry if I woke you. Just got a drink of water. Go back to sleep." Later, soft patting of slippers pacing the hallway woke me, but I stayed where I was. Mom had a lot on her mind.

Sleep arrived in time to allow me a few hours rest before a ray of sunlight struck me in the eye at eight a.m.

I stumbled to the kitchen to make coffee but found a full pot in the coffeemaker. I filled a cup and waited for my mother to hang up the phone.

She glanced my way, so I asked, "Chad?"

"Yes. I gave him a quick rundown—just the basics—so he wouldn't be taken by surprise when the talk starts to circulate. I thought he might have heard already. The gossip chain must be slow today."

"How did he react?"

"Very quietly. You know how he likes to think things over before he speaks. Then he sputtered a bit about it being early for April fool's jokes. I told him it was no joke but not to worry about it, we'd talk this afternoon."

My poor brother. "Yeah, right. Don't worry about it. His brain is probably whirling. I'm still trying to understand, and I witnessed it." I pulled bread from the cupboard. "Do you want toast?"

~~

After breakfast and a visit to the police station to make an official statement, my mother accompanied me to my house. We stood on the porch assessing the damage. I'd prepared myself for the broken latch and the bullet hole, but what I saw took my breath away. I must have been in shock when we left the night before. "It's so much worse than I thought. Even the windows are shattered." I'd been fond of the little diamond shaped windows on top of the door.

We stepped inside. Bits of glass mixed with the splintered wood littering the foyer. And dirt. And a few rocks. "Who brought in all the mud?" I paced to the kitchen closet, pulled out the broom and started sweeping.

My mother stood watching me, with her hands on her

hips. I shrugged. "I don't know what else to do. At least it will look cleaner." I needed to keep my hands busy rather than contemplate the next few days. There would be calls to the insurance company. Forms to fill out. I hated filling out claim forms. How would I get the door—and the bathroom closet—repaired? Would I be able to find a repairman? The few handymen in Twin Fawn were always busy.

And then the thought I tried to push away. There would be more meetings with the police. Serious talks. What would become of my mother?

I jumped at the sound of footsteps on the sidewalk. The sweepings scattered and I raised the broom over my head, ready to swing. Garrett Reed laughed and put a hand up. "Don't shoot. I come in peace. Arnie said you had trouble here last night and might need some carpenter work." He carried a toolbox.

My cheeks got hot as I lowered my broom. "I'm so sorry, Garrett. I have a lot on my mind, and I guess I'm a little jumpy."

My stomach got fluttery at Garrett's smile and the warmth in his eyes. His kind voice almost brought on tears. "Not a problem. You have a right to be on edge."

He examined the splintered frame before glancing up at me. "Arnie was right. You definitely need some repair work. You won't feel safe in this house until it's fixed."

He stuck a finger in the bullet hole. "Looks like this must have been exciting."

It wasn't a question, so I just smiled. If I'd tried to fill him in on the events of the previous evening, I might have fallen into his arms, sobbing. I held my breath and nodded. "I'm grateful to you for coming. I'll pay you whatever it costs."

"I don't want any money for it. You're in need. That's why I'm here." He winked and pivoted to return to his pickup. "I'll get the new door from the truck."

A new door? With a sigh of relief and a smile on my face, I went back to sweeping the foyer. My mother came from the kitchen and leaned out the door in time to see Garrett return to his vehicle. I told her of his kind intentions.

She nodded in his direction. "There's a good young man. Kind, handy, and handsome. All the traits that make a good husband."

I stopped sweeping to gaze at her. "Now I know you've lost your mind. You have never encouraged me to get to know Garrett. You know you've always discouraged it. What's happened that, all of a sudden, he's a good catch?"

"Everything has changed. Now that you know my story, I don't have to keep the secret. I had good reason to be afraid that you would get close to Garrett. At least, I considered it a good reason."

"I thought you told me everything last night." A chill ran up my spine. "You didn't mention Garrett. What other secret are we talking about?"

She leaned on the door frame between the foyer and living room. "Let's sit in the living room while that young man works. I have more to explain."

I propped the broom against the wall and followed her, wondering how many secrets one sweet librarian could harbor. "I'm not sure if I can handle any more revelations."

"This is minor compared to what you already know." She kicked off her shoes and curled up in the big armchair.

I took my place on the sofa and steeled myself for whatever she had in store. "Okay. Shoot." I winced. I guess that was a poor choice of words.

My mother took a breath and began. "From the day I'd arrived in Twin Fawn there was one person I always thought might know the truth about me. He was the sheriff. During my first couple of weeks, I caught him following me. Everywhere I went, I'd look up and he would be there —across the street, in the post office, or on the road. I hoped that it was common police procedure for when a stranger arrived in town. As I said before, I'd become pretty good at creating scenarios to cope with anything that scared me."

She paused long enough to shrug and continued. "I learned to portray a respected member of the community, being nice to everyone and so polite I hardly recognized myself. I got a job at the library right away. That's where I met your father. He came in to return some books. Then he walked back in almost every day for books he didn't even need. I recognized a good man when I saw him. And a safe man. It didn't take long for us to start dating. He took me to church on our first date."

Mom closed her eyes and took a deep breath. I knew something hard was coming. "One day the sheriff showed up while I sat alone in the diner. He pulled up a chair at my table. That scared me. I thought my greatest fear had finally materialized. Then he came right out and asked me if I'd been involved in the crime spree in Evelynton."

Mom fanned herself with her hand. "It was as if he'd hit me in the face. My mouth hung open. All I could do was shake my head. When I found my voice, I told him I had no idea what he was talking about. God forgive me,

I could still lie. To him and to myself."

"How did he know?"

"I guess he'd been interested in that case. He knew someone on the Evelynton police force and had heard they'd been embarrassed chasing a group of kids."

"He let me know, in no uncertain terms, that Twin Fawn was known for their low crime rate and he wanted to keep it that way. I'll never forget his words. He looked me straight in the eyes and said, 'Gerald Cassell is a friend of mine. I would hate to see him hurt. So, watch yourself. I don't expect any new crime in my town.' He could have burned a hole right through me with that stare."

"That was it? Just the warning?"

She nodded. "I never talked to him again. Never even looked at him when we passed on the street. I hoped if I acted innocent, he'd be convinced. Or maybe he wouldn't want to hurt your father by arresting me."

Not long after I married Gerald, the sheriff resigned and left town. But his ex-wife and son still lived here in Twin Fawn, so I never felt completely safe. That sheriff was Garrett's father, Jack Reed."

I stared at her. "Garrett's father, a policeman? I didn't know. You never mentioned it."

"No, I wouldn't have. Because as Garrett got older, I was afraid Jack might share his suspicions about me. What would I have done if Garrett told you?"

"Mother, I can't believe you have lived with this fear for so many years."

"As I mentioned, I learned to compartmentalize. Shoved it far back in my mind. And now that you know the truth, I have nothing to hide." She smiled the first real smile I'd seen from her in the last two days. "The truth set me free."

"I confessed everything to Arnie this morning, and he will get in touch with the Evelynton police department. He'll let me know what the next step is." Mother sighed and relaxed into the chair.

I didn't feel quite as calm as my mother and couldn't sit still any longer. I got up and went to the foyer to inspect Garrett's progress on the door. "Wow. You're almost finished. I can't tell you how much I appreciate this. It looks great."

Garrett grinned, once again revealing his dimples. "I'm happy to help. And my next project is your mother's apartment." He stepped past me to the living room and spoke to her. "Mrs. Cassell, as soon as I finish here, I'll head over to your apartment. Do you have time to meet me there?"

Mom jumped up from her chair. "Garrett Reed, it's so nice of you to do this for us. I'll get right over there and put on a pot of coffee. And I have a fresh batch of chocolate chip cookies in the cookie jar."

Garrett flashed a grin. "Great. Your cookies are famous."

Why hadn't I thought of feeding him coffee and cookies? This must be why all the men liked my mother.

I hovered while Garrett continued putting the finishing touches on my door, only distracted by a black pickup truck at the curb. The occupant climbed out and sauntered up the walk. A distinguished man, tall—about Garrett's height. Thick, silver hair set off his dark eyes.

Garrett glanced up from his work. "Hi, Dad. Libby, this is my father, Jack Reed."

The man nodded to me. I reached out and shook his hand but remained silent, my heart pounding out of control. Garrett's father? The policeman.

Mr. Reed showed dimples to match Garrett's as he spoke to his son. "I'm glad I got here before you finished. I planned to go to work on Katherine's place with you."

The man focused on my mother, who had stepped up beside me. "Hello Katherine. Do you remember me?"

My mother stared at the man for a moment, then put her hand to her forehead. "Sheriff Reed. How are you? How long has it been? I remember seeing you at Gerald's funeral, though I didn't get a chance to talk to you."

"Yes, I had to leave right after the service that day. It's been a long while, but you haven't aged a bit. As beautiful as ever."

My mother laughed and blushed a little on this rare occasion where she seemed to be at a loss for words.

"And I'm just Jack. Not a sheriff anymore. Retired some years back."

My mother seemed to still be speechless, so he continued. "I hope you don't mind. Arnie, at the station, told me about your recent trouble. Didn't get to Twin Fawn in time to help Garrett with this project but I thought I'd help him work on your place. We'll make sure your new door is sturdy."

Mom had composed herself. "That would be so nice of you. I know you'll do a good job. And I see you've raised your son well. Come in and sit with me while Garrett finishes up here. Let's talk."

Jack wiped his shoes on the mat and followed my mother. "Just what I came to do. I need to speak to you, now that this is all over. I'd always wished I'd been able to explain things before I left town."

Electricity sparked between them, causing me to feel I was intruding. I retreated to the living room. When

Mom brought Jack in, they sat on the sofa and didn't seem to notice me in the corner chair. I thought it might be awkward to get up and sneak out. Besides, I wanted to be close in case Mom needed me.

"I don't remember exactly when you left town, or why. Everyone thought it was probably because of your divorce."

"I left about the time you married Gerald Cassell. And I hadn't been divorced from Garrett's mother very long. Always regretted how things worked out. Everything was complicated. And then Gerald proposed."

"I'd made a point of following you when you arrived in Twin Fawn. Partly because I'd heard some rumors about the crime spree in Evelynton and knew that's where you were from. But mostly I followed you because you were the most beautiful woman I'd ever seen."

Tears sprang to my eyes. I scooted my chair back and tried to become invisible. Searching my pockets for a tissue, I wondered if Garrett would age as well as his father had.

Jack continued. "Couldn't tell you how I felt. Not with what I suspected about your past. Talk about being conflicted, I would have protected you forever. I figured Cassell was a good man. He'd take care of you. The job offer came at the perfect time. I grabbed it and left town."

My mother and Jack Reed gazed into each other's eyes. There I sat, a voyeur listening in on a conversation straight out of a romance novel.

"When I stopped you at the diner, you were scared, so I figured I'd been right about your involvement in that trouble. It broke my heart to let you know I was on to you and to have to threaten you. I wish I could have done more for you, then."

"You were just doing your job. And you could have arrested me. I probably would have confessed. Already felt so guilty. Fortunately, your warning pushed me along. I had already begun to turn myself around and would never break the law again."

Mom smiled her sweet smile at the man gazing into her eyes. "Jack, tell me about your life. How have you been?"

"I've had a good life, though I never remarried. Leaving town didn't help get you out of my mind. I compared every woman I met to you. They didn't stand a chance."

He paused and took a breath. "I've been gone long enough. Retired last year, and now I'm moving back to be closer to Garrett and some old friends. I spoke to Arnie about your visit this morning. If there's anything I can help with when you deal with the ramifications, I will. If you want, I'll go with you to Evelynton to turn yourself in.

"Thank you, Jack. It would be nice to have a strong arm to lean on."

I slumped into the chair forgetting for a moment where I was. I sighed—loudly—thinking how nice it would be to meet a man so gallant.

Chapter Twenty

Mom switched off her phone and slid it into her pocket while returning to her seat across from me. I wanted to bombard her with questions, but busied myself with smoothing her fresh white tablecloth to give her time. She seemed lost in her thoughts, mulling over serious matters.

Finally, when I could wait no longer, I got her attention. "Mom. What's going on?"

She glanced at me and smiled, almost as though she'd forgotten I sat at her kitchen table. "That was Loretta, the manager of Clairmont Retirement Village, on the phone. She is such a nice woman. Always helpful and kind. I know it was hard for her, but she informed me that some of the residents called an emergency meeting last night. It seems the majority sentiment is that I move out. I could tell she felt bad about it and she wanted me to know that everyone loved me. They've decided that my lifestyle isn't in tune with the community."

Mother let out a short laugh. "She went on to explain they've noticed I'm much busier than all the others. I suspect it took some time to come up with a reason that didn't actually say they aren't accustomed to madmen beating on doors in the middle of the night. I can't say I blame the residents. Most of them are old and frail. They moved to Clairmont for peace and quiet, not the kind of excitement we had."

Her eyes widened as she continued. "They gave me four weeks to find another place."

I leaned across the table. "Four weeks? Only a month? That isn't fair. Don't you have a lease or something?"

"I do, but I guess there's some kind of provision for this type of thing. It has to do with noise regulations and parties. They seem to think it covers my case."

Unable to sit still, I slid my chair back, got up and paced around the table. "Still, where's the loyalty? The Christian kindness? Has the manager seen the door? It's in better shape than it was before the—incident"

Mother reached out to touch my arm. "Sit down, dear. Think about it from their point of view."

I let out a breath. "Okay, I guess this is a special case. That kind of disturbance isn't what they expect anywhere in Twin Fawn, let alone a retirement village."

In truth, the manager's decision hadn't surprised me. I'd already considered the possibility there would be ramifications and had been mentally sorting through possible living arrangements. Twin Fawn didn't offer much of a selection.

I slid back into my chair. "What are you going to do? How are we going to find a place in such a short time?"

For the first time, my mother's forehead crinkled into serious wrinkle lines. "I don't know. I suppose I'll check the paper for apartments. Maybe you can ask Clair. She may have listings of rentals. Of course, I realize there aren't many choices in Twin Fawn. And what are the chances that one is available?"

I did a quick debate with myself. Should I be as generous as I knew my mother would be in an instance like this? Or should I protect my privacy as a single woman? The good daughter won and I put on my bright face. "Mother, why are we even considering apartments? I have plenty of room at the house. Why don't you move back in with me?"

Mom tilted her head and glanced at me. I could tell she now debated the living arrangements. I hadn't considered the fact that she might prefer living alone. I charged ahead. "You can have the downstairs bedroom. Easy to get to. No stairs. I've actually been thinking of remodeling the two upstairs bedrooms. The smaller one would make a great dressing room/closet. I'd redecorate the larger for my bedroom."

"That's very kind, Liberty. But an awful inconvenience for you."

"No, I won't hear of you moving into some rental when I have extra space. You know when you decided on Clairmont, there were no apartments half as nice."

To my surprise, I began to look forward to a new roommate. "You'll live with me. It will be fun. Let's redecorate the downstairs room for you. New paint, curtains, bedding."

I confess my mind was also busy thinking that if any more of my mother's old acquaintances showed up, I wanted to be aware.

Mom put an elbow on the table and rested her chin in her hand. "It is an attractive invitation. Let's pray about it today and talk again this evening. Meanwhile, I'll begin packing things I don't use regularly."

~~

I threw a pile of clothes into the washing machine and noticed dust bunnies between the washer and dryer. I needed to get a thorough cleaning done before my mother moved in. Only a week left before moving day. Would we combine our laundry or do separate loads? As I contemplated that big question, my new doorbell rang.

I released the deadbolt to find my friend Clair on the porch. "Hey. How was your trip?"

She planted both hands on her hips. "Liberty Breeze, I leave you alone for three weeks and you manage to get into a calamity. Sharon Smith left an ominous message on my phone."

"Sharon who?"

"You know the Smiths." Clair raised her arm and pointed. "They are your neighbors two doors down. Remember, I helped them find the house."

I glanced in that direction. "Oh, right. They are rarely outside the house. I'm surprised they noticed anything going on here. What did she say?"

"She sounded a little distraught and asked me what kind of neighborhood I got them into. She said something about a shoot-out over here."

The scene flashed through my mind and the fear I'd experienced came back for a moment. I quickly conjured up my calm face. "That's stretching it a bit. I wouldn't call it a shoot-out. I mean there was a gun involved. But only one. My mother shot it and didn't hit anything but my front door. I admit the guy made a lot of noise trying to break in."

I gazed over Clair's shoulder and scanned the empty street. "All the neighbors have been kind of quiet since, but they'll get over it. The residents at Clairmont Retirement Village, on the other hand, may need trauma counseling."

Clair's eyes grew wide, and wrinkles snaked across her forehead. "You're telling me someone tried to break in. And your sweet mother shot a hole in your door? One of us is delirious, because none of this sounds right."

I smiled, hoping to ease her mind. "Come in. I'll give you the whole scoop. Then maybe you'll be able to correct some of the farfetched rumors that will be coming your way."

"I can't wait to hear this story." Clair followed me through the foyer. "I like the new door, by the way."

I led the way into the living room. "Sit down and have some popcorn. Just made it. I'll get us something to drink."

"Awesome, I'm hungry."

When I got back with the drinks, Clair had the popcorn bowl cradled like a baby. "What in the world happened?"

"I'll tell you everything, but no questions until I'm finished. I don't want to get confused on the sequence of events." I began at the beginning, striving to be as clear as possible. Since Clair had been out of town, I'd had no one to hear my inmost thoughts. Holding in my deep fears had been a struggle. But with the relief of unloading the horrors of that night, my words began to tumble out. I spoke faster and faster, creating sort of an avalanche. Clair interrupted more than once to urge me to slow down. By the end of my tale, she hadn't touched the popcorn.

I took time to breathe, and my friend stared at me. "By the time you're our age, you think you have a grip on reality. Then it blows up in your face."

I nodded. "I grew up thinking I knew my peaceful

little family. A fairytale life. But obviously, it was only a fairytale. I would never have dreamed my mother could shoot a gun. Now, she tells me she's an excellent marksman. And I discovered she isn't as frail as I thought. The woman's certainly not one to panic in an emergency."

"Those are two revelations that will take time to process." Clair paused to put the popcorn bowl on the coffee table. "You said she wanted to confess everything. How's that going?

"We went to Evelynton to talk to the police and told them the whole story. Garrett's dad, Jack, went with us. He's retired law enforcement and came back in town to help. Oh, that's another story I'll have to tell you, sometime. He proved to be a great help. Incidentally, I think they're dating, now."

Clair stared at me, but didn't respond.

I continued. "It took the Evelynton authorities forever to dig up the old case files. I think they would have preferred it if she'd stayed in hiding. Officer Farlow kept sputtering something about statute of limitations and the ton of paperwork involved."

"But Mom insisted. Surprisingly, she convinced a judge to sentence her to the same punishment the other young gang members served back then. Gotta love small towns. She'll get community service projects in both Evelynton and Twin Fawn. The attorney said she would have to drive to Evelynton twice a month to do her community service."

"She's already started. She went to the high school to meet with the kids. Mom insisted her service include talking to high school kids about using their natural creativity to benefit the community instead of causing trouble. She loves helping them find volunteer service projects."

"And Pastor Prescott is in charge of her service while in Twin Fawn. You know she's right where she belongs. Helping other people. She'll be doing exactly what she's been doing all along, but without the guilt."

"The pastor finally convinced her that she had been forgiven since she confessed her belief in Jesus and made him Lord of her life. She realized that repenting meant changing her ways, as she had already done. What she couldn't accept is that Jesus' forgiveness had always been there. She never had to earn it."

Clair wiped a tear from her eye. "Sweet Katherine has felt guilty all this time? I don't know of another person in Twin Fawn who is as—Christian as she is."

"There's more." I grabbed some tissues from a side table and handed them to Clair. "As another part of her repentance, she is intent on talking to Bernie, the man who tried to break in. I tried to talk her out of it. He's in jail and still really angry. It's doubtful that he'll be receptive, but she wants to ask for his forgiveness. And then she'll share with him that he, too, can be forgiven. Even though he'll be spending more time in jail, she wants him to know he can have peace in his life."

Clair glanced at the popcorn bowl and grabbed a handful to stuff into her mouth.

"And one more thing. With all that confessing, I remembered I'd been hiding something, too. You know I'd been keeping our trip to Evelynton a secret. So, one day when we were talking, I told Mom all about it. Particularly about our chat with Peggy Clooney Larkin. As soon as she heard how unhappy Peggy had become, she put her on the list to visit."

Clair focused a glassy-eyed stare at me and continued to stuff popcorn into her mouth. Between bites, she said, "I'm never leaving town again.

Chapter Twenty-One

I closed the computer and stretched my arms high, releasing the kinks in my back. The previous day's sales had produced a healthy batch of receipts, taking me longer than expected to get them entered into the system. Time to escape my tiny claustrophobic office.

A bubbly laugh rang through the store, followed by a manly snicker. I had to smile. "Perfect timing." My friend Clair had arrived. I knew few people who could laugh as often and freely as Clair. She loved joking with Mr. Bennett. A glance out to the sales floor confirmed it. The two stood with their heads together, still giggling.

I grabbed my bag and scooted around the desk to greet my friend. "What are you two laughing about this time?"

My boss held a clip board to his chest and gazed at me over the top of his wirerimmed glasses while hiccupping a laugh. He glanced at Clair, laying a hand on her shoulder. "Wait, let me tell it." Pivoting toward me and standing up straight, he announced. "What is the opposite of a croissant?" He took a moment to pause, giving dramatic effect before shouting the answer. "A happy uncle!"

I slapped my hand over my eyes and couldn't stifle

the groan. I shook my head at the two. "That's really awful."

Still laughing, Mr. Bennett said, "I don't know where Clair gets such witticisms."

Clair poked him in the shoulder. "I get them from my clients and save the best for you."

Still grinning, Mr. Bennett asked, "Where are you ladies going for lunch today?"

I shrugged and glanced at my friend. "It's your turn to choose. What do you think?"

"Let's go to The Caffeinated Cup. I'm in the mood for their cranberry walnut salad," Clair chirped. "And I'm dying for a hot cup of coffee."

"Sounds good to me. We can have their Legendary Chocolate Layer Cake for dessert."

I twisted toward my boss. "Shall I bring you something, Mr. Bennett?"

"Thank you, Libby, but I don't need a thing. Packed my lunch today. While it's quiet in here, I'll turn to the fifties station on the radio and enjoy my lunch."

"Okay. Call me if you change your mind. I'll be back in an hour." I skirted past him and followed Clair who was already three steps ahead of me on her way out the door.

My boss waved. "You take all the time you want. Have a nice time."

We joined the lunch crowd on the sidewalk and were out of Stanley's earshot when Clair lowered her voice. "He's cute for an older guy. It's too bad it didn't work out with your mom. I bet he's disappointed that she and Jack Reed are spending time together."

"I'm not sure if Stanley's disappointed that Mom's dating someone else, or that she is not the woman he imagined her to be. Maybe he's relieved. Can you see Mr. Bennett with a woman who owns two guns, is a crack shot, and has proved she can stare down a raging criminal?"

"I see what you mean. She might be more woman than he wants to deal with. I really can't imagine Stanley trying to keep up with her, and the gun ownership thing is probably more than he bargained for." Clair giggled.

"No kidding. It's definitely more than I bargained for."

I scanned the area to make sure no one was close enough to overhear. "He doesn't even know the whole story. The Twin Fawn gossips never picked up the really juicy bits. Thank goodness the police managed to keep most of the details quiet."

We stood at the corner waiting for traffic to clear. "I'm sort of sorry that I lobbied for the relationship. Should never have encouraged him, but they really seemed to be a perfect match. How wrong could I be? Now I understand why she always managed to avoid him. Never would I have thought that Stanley Bennett would be too mild mannered to interest my mother—the librarian."

Clair strode ahead and waved an index finger. "I meet a lot of people in my real estate business. I'll keep my eyes open for a nice quiet single lady for him."

Having reached another corner, Clair grabbed my arm, and we scooted across the street before the next line of cars approached. "I can understand why Jack Reed attracts her. Did I hear that since he's retired, he's been doing some private detective work on the side?"

"Yes, that's what Mom told me. I have to say I'm glad most of his work is in Indianapolis, not Twin Fawn.

I don't want her to get involved in it."

Clair glanced at me. "Why not? It sounds exciting."

"Would you want your mother sitting all night in a stakeout and spying on people or chasing criminals trying to serve warrants?"

"Would she really do that?"

I shrugged. "I wouldn't be surprised at anything she decided to do."

Clair pulled open the door of The Caffeinated Cup and allowed me to enter first. "Grab that table by the window. I'll put in our order." I did as I was told and settled at the two-topper to watch people out on the street.

Clair returned to set my coffee on the table and took a seat across from me. "How's Katherine getting along since all the excitement has died down?"

"Better than ever. Now that Mom has told me her story and confessed to the authorities, she is a new woman. It's unbelievable how much she's loosened up. She laughs more. She's still doing all her volunteer work but seems to be more vigorous than ever. She even found time to sign up for Salsa dance lessons at the city center."

"Salsa dancing? Along with all her community service work? Where does she get her energy?"

"She tells me that the truth has set her free. Keeping old secrets carried more weight than she realized."

The barista called Clair's name. I glanced over my shoulder to see our lunch plates at the counter. "I'll get them." I grabbed the tray from the counter and brought it to our table. "A group of dancers meets at Morelli's Irish Pub every Thursday evening for Salsa dancing as well as some good old rock and roll." I did a little hip swaying before I settled in my chair. "Maybe we should join them sometime."

Clair froze with her fork in the air. "Maybe we'll just go and watch."

I glanced around the room, sort of regretting the attempted dance moves. "Yeah, you're right."

After making short work of my salad, I leaned back in my chair to stare at the citizens on the sidewalk. Some carrying shopping bags. Others laughing together as they walked. "This is such a peaceful little town. I love watching the cars go by. Imagine all those happy families living their simple lives, running errands. Taking their kids to the park. What a sweet, lovely town we live in."

Clair smiled. "Aren't you the romantic." She turned to peer out the window as well. "Wait." She leaned forward and gazed at a line of cars waiting at the stoplight.

"Do you see that gray car?" Clair pointed, and I put my elbows on the table to follow her gaze. "Third one back. Does the driver look familiar?"

"I can't see the driver." I stood and stepped close to the window. "Nope. You must have better eyesight than I have.

Clair stood beside me. "It's a woman. And looks like …." The light turned green and the traffic traveled on.

Clair returned to the table and plopped into her chair. "Forget it. I'm imagining things. I thought the driver looked sort of familiar but really, they were too far away to see clearly."

I turned to gather our dishes. "Who did you think you saw?"

My friend leaned back and waved a hand. "No one. Guess I forgot where I was. Silly me, thinking there might be another troublemaker in Twin Fawn."

I laughed. "Troublemaker? No, not Twin Fawn. I love this town." I hoisted my bag onto my shoulder. "I've probably been away from the store long enough. I hope Stanley hasn't been swamped with customers."

Before we left, I picked up a to-go order of chocolate cake for my boss. Catching Clair's eye, I shrugged. "Still trying to make amends."

We left the Caffeinated Cup and bid good-bye on the sidewalk. Clair trotted to her office, and I enjoyed a leisurely stroll back to Bennett's Hardware. All was well in the world. A wholesome community, good friends, and chocolate. What could be more comforting?

As for troublemakers? No way. Clair was surely off her rocker.

Chapter Twenty-Two

Left on my own, thoughts quickly turned to worry about poor Mr. Bennett. The man led a lonely life. As far as I could tell, the hardware store occupied his entire life. He never mentioned friends. How could I cheer him? I had no gift for telling jokes like Clair.

He needed company. A selection of faces appeared in my mind. Elderly, single women who might fit the bill. I'd chosen a few before my heels dug into the sidewalk, bringing my stroll and thoughts to a screeching halt. Was I crazy? Had recent experience taught me nothing? I'd been convinced my mother was perfect for him, but obviously I hadn't had a clue as to her true personality. What made me think I could be a matchmaker? The next attempt might be even more disastrous.

I entered the hardware store wallowing in those depressing thoughts, and shoved the door shut with a bang. I'd used more force than necessary. "Oops." My boss stood in the first aisle wielding a broom and dustpan. Fortunately, I'd brought a gift. If he'd heard the door slam, he forgave me as soon as I handed him his slice of the Legendary Chocolate Layer Cake.

"This is just the thing. I'll be back to finish the sweeping. Leave the broom where it is." Parking the broom in the aisle, he took his prize and scurried to the back room.

Taking a clue from the boss, I stashed my bag in the bottom drawer of my desk and found a dust cloth to use on my office. Mr. Bennett must have enjoyed the cake, because it wasn't long before he took up the broom again and quietly sang to the vintage toons on the radio.

I polished the file cabinets and pondered where I could buy a joke book. That bright idea deflated as soon as I remembered how jokes and funny stories die an ugly death by poor delivery.

Mr. Bennett sang, lost in his chores. I dusted, lost in my thoughts. But we both snapped to attention when a car, with siren blaring, sped past. I stepped out of my office and glanced at Mr. Bennett. "Was that a police car?" Before he could answer, we witnessed a second squad car chasing the first. We trotted to the front of the store to press our faces against the window.

Mr. Bennett twisted toward me. "Well, that doesn't happen very often. What do you think they're up to?"

I widened my eyes and shrugged. "My guess is they're late for lunch." It had been a well-worn joke that the only time the Twin Fawn police sirens were used was when the officers were late for an appointment.

Pedestrians, who had stopped to watch, continued their journey. Activity on the street returned to normal. We moved away from the window to resume tidying the store. I straightened shelves, occasionally glancing back to the street in hopes of catching something interesting. I noticed Mr. Bennett did the same. But all seemed quiet. I remembered the unfinished dusting and returned to my office.

I hadn't finished with the cabinets when a man's

voice thundered through the store. I admit being surprised when I peeked out to see Lloyd Hamilton standing in the doorway of the hardware store with more color in his complexion than usual. I'd never heard him raise his voice in public, or at any time, for that matter.

He shouted to Mr. Bennett. "There's something going on down at the library. Some kind of commotion. Did you see the two squad cars traveling in that direction?"

Stanley called after him. "I sure saw 'em. What kind of commotion do you think it might be? Is it a health emergency?" I didn't hear Lloyd's answer. He had already returned to the sidewalk, taking long strides in the direction of the library.

I stared at Mr. Bennett. "The library?" My heart began a rhythmic thump against the wall of my chest. "Mother is working. Some of the workers are elderly. My mother is elderly. Do you think someone had a heart attack? Or maybe fell while reaching for the higher bookshelves? It would be just like Mom to push her luck on the ladder."

I returned to my desk and grabbed my handbag. On the way to the front door, I called. "I'm going over there. I have a…bad feeling." It was time I paid attention to the intuition my mom insisted was mine if I would only listen.

I stood on the street searching my bag for keys, but took off on foot when I remembered leaving the car at home. Fortunately, I always wore comfortable shoes and could travel at a good pace. Having grown up in Twin Fawn, I knew all the short cuts. I ran through two allies and one private lawn to get to the scene.

The sight was worse than I'd expected. Two squad

cars, parked diagonally across the street, blocked access to the library. Uniformed officers stood on either side with arms spread to keep onlookers away. I stood in the crowd for a minute before losing patience. As soon as I spotted Arnie, I jogged to the line. A policeman eyed me and mouthed the word "No." I nodded, head-faked to the left, then cut to the right to duck under his arm. When I reached Arnie without being tackled, I felt like I'd reached home base and grabbed his arm. "Arnie, what has happened? Is someone hurt?"

Surprise registered on his face and then resignation as he recognized me. "To soon to tell. We don't have all the facts yet." He put his hands on my shoulders and gave me a gentle nudge. "Keep back Libby. We've been told someone has a weapon. There was a report of a gunshot. You don't want to get in the middle of it. It would be best if you moved back across the street. The situation could accelerate at any moment."

I dug in my heels. "I'm not leaving. My mother's working today."

"I'm sorry, Libby." I could tell he debated whether to tell me. Finally, he said, "Some of the people got out. They said there's a crazy woman in there waving a gun around." He leveled his gaze at me. I'm not sure why he felt he had to add, "A stranger, not Katherine." He pointed toward a small group of women clustered behind a squad car. "The few library patrons who escaped reported they'd never seen this woman. She let them leave but kept some hostages."

I turned and searched the group, then did a double-take. My boss stood in the center. Two women clung to him while he patted their backs. I tore my attention away and turned back to Arnie. "Um, did Mom get out? Have you seen her?"

"No, Libby. I'm afraid Mrs. Cassell must still be inside."

An explosion reverberated around the building and rattled my brain. Arnie hit the ground and pulled me with him. I stared at him. "Was that a bomb?"

"No, a gunshot. It looks like a shot out window beside the door."

I pulled myself up so my head and shoulders extended over the trunk of the police car. Sure enough, one of the windows had shattered. Broken glass littered the ground.

Arnie grabbed the collar of my shirt and pulled me back behind the car. "Stay down!"

I remained crouched beside him dreading the next shot, then shrieked when I felt a tap on my arm. Pulling in a breath, I glanced over my shoulder. Not the gun-wielding brute who had flashed through my mind. "Clair! How did you get in here?"

"Probably the same way you did. A little creativity and a lot of determination. Tell me what's happening. Is Katherine alright?"

With my friend at my side, I lost all false bravery. I felt tears stinging my eyes and could only manage a shrug. After a few deep breaths, an answer surfaced. "My mom's still in there. They say a crazy woman—not Mom—is holding a gun on them. She just shot out that window."

Clair turned to Arnie. "I think I know who it is. It's…."

A sigh and squinted eyes said the man wasn't interested in information from the general public. "I don't have time to talk to you now Mrs. Berry." That was a lie. He did have time. All the police officers had been sitting behind the squad cars, with their hands in their pockets. Arnie had nowhere to go, so Clair told him about Peggy Clooney, the very unhappy woman from Katherine Cassell's past.

"I'm pretty sure I saw her driving through town earlier today."

I stared at Clair. "Why didn't you tell me you saw Peggy?"

My friend shrugged. "I almost did, but I could have been mistaken. I thought I'd imagined it. You know I'm sometimes overly suspicious."

I shook my head. "I can't believe it's Peggy. I know she seemed unhappy but would that be enough to drive all the way here with a gun? I know I first thought the woman was mentally ill. But after some thought, I decided she had probably been having a bad day when we talked to her."

"Libby, you are just like your mother. Unwilling to see anything but good in people. I think that woman seemed to be having more than a bad day. She showed signs of being emotionally and mentally disturbed."

Clair turned back to Arnie. "If I'm right there's no telling what she might do."

Arnie must have decided to take a chance on Clair's theory. It took him only a moment to make a call into the station asking them to check on any priors in the name of Peggy or Margaret Clooney.

We waited. There were no more gunshots. No sound at all came from the library. Slowly, policemen got off the ground and began to stand, staying behind their vehicles and keeping a safe distance from the building.

Arnie pulled a blowhorn from his car and began

broadcasting demands. "You don't want to hurt anyone, um, Peggy. Toss your gun out. Release the hostages and then come out with your hands up."

Arnie seemed a little confused about how to handle the situation but I remembered he'd probably never had any experience other than television.

My legs were cramped. I stood and paced from one end of the police car to the other and then back again. On my second circuit, my cell phone rang. I dug it from my bag. Mom's name appeared on the screen.

At my answer, she spoke three words. "Send Arnie up."

"Mom. Are you alright? What's happening? What can I do?" As I threw questions at her, I heard only the click of her phone. She'd hung up on me.

I delivered the message. Arnie seemed anything but confident at the request. But after a moment's contemplation, he set his jaw and gave a stiff nod. He immediately left the safety of the squad car and slipped up to the library. The heavy wooden door opened a crack.

Arnie conversed with someone inside. He alternately shook his head and nodded until the door closed. Then he whirled around and descended the stairs. He first spoke to the other police officers, then returned to the spot where Clair and I waited. Arnie glanced at Clair. "You were right. Mrs. Cassell called the woman, Peggy."

He turned to me. "Katherine wants us to let them have some time. She's reasoning with the woman."

"Are you crazy? That's my mother in there. They've already had time. How can you let a crazy woman have more time when she has a gun and has proved she will use it?" I'd never thought of myself as a hysterical person, but recent events had brought out a certain amount of hysteria.

Arnie shrugged. "Mrs. Cassell said Peggy was never aiming at anyone. Just trying to get some attention. Your mother's positive she can resolve the situation."

Mom had always displayed a certain gift for turning people to her way of thinking. Was she using her gift to persuade Peggy or Arnie?"

Arnie reached inside his car and pulled out a candy bar. As he tore open the wrapper, he offered Clair and me a bite. We declined the offer. He leaned on the car while he ate.

We waited. I paced while Clair sat on the curb. Minutes ticked by. Then an hour. It could have been two hours or more. I lost track of time. Then, the murmur of the crowd grew louder.

All eyes were on the library door as it opened. My mother poked her head out. She held her hands in the air and shouted. "Don't shoot. I'm all right and Peggy is coming out peaceably." Mom stepped carefully down the steps with Peggy close behind. "Please don't hurt her. She's surrendering. She's very sorry. Just having a mood. You know how it is."

When Peggy and my mother reached the sidewalk, Arnie and his officers surrounded them. Someone placed handcuffs on Peggy.

Clair and I were right behind Arnie. I grabbed my mother's shoulders and looked at her from head to foot. There were smudges of dirt on her slacks and a scrape or two on her hands. "What happened to you?"

"Oh, it's nothing." Mom reached behind her, produced a gun from her waistband and handed it to Arnie. "I thought I'd better get this away from her. We had a little tussle."

Chapter Twenty-Three

I'd been counting the lines on the floor. Shadows created by the sun pouring through the lone window in the office. Shifting from side to side in attempt to find a comfortable spot in my chair and ease my aching back. How did my mother cope? Her back muscles were twenty years older than mine. The Twin Fawn police department hadn't splurged on seating for the interview room. Definitely not provided for comfort.

Mom had given her detailed statement at least an hour ago. Now we waited for the copy she would be asked to sign. The officer had promised to return shortly. How long could it take? The two of us sat in silence, having exhausted all topics of conversation.

I searched for something new to talk about. Anything to break the monotony. "Why do you suppose they paint all their offices gray? I think it causes the room to be dark, don't you?"

Mom gazed around the room, gave a tired smile and shrugged. "It is a bit depressing. They could use a picture for interest. A landscape. Anything to lighten the mood. Maybe, after this is over, we can suggest a new color scheme. I bet it would make their work easier."

A tap on the door drew our attention. Arnie swung it

open. "Sorry to have been so long, Mrs. Cassell. The secretary is out today. It took a while to get a copy without typos. Please check this over and make sure we got everything right and I haven't left anything out. Then sign on that line at the bottom."

Mom beamed a smile at him exhibiting an unexpected spurt of energy. "I'm sure it's fine. Thank you for your diligence, Officer." She scanned the document, signed it, and handed it back to him.

As we left the building, I leaned toward my mother. "You didn't even read it, did you?"

She made a quick glance behind us and whispered. "No. I would have signed my death warrant to get out of there."

We stepped to the sidewalk as a black BMW pulled to the curb. The tinted window lowered, revealing Clair's sweet smile. "Need a ride?"

"Clair Barry, you are a life saver." I leaned in the open window. "How did you know we were finished? I hope you weren't waiting out here all this time."

Clair grinned. "It's nice to have connections." She gestured toward the police station. "I helped one of the guys get a house last month, so he was kind enough to text me when you were almost finished. I didn't think you'd be up to walking home. Hop in."

My mother crawled into the back seat while I took the front. Beyond our thanks for my friend's thoughtfulness, we couldn't muster enough energy for conversation.

I had almost dozed off when Clair pulled into the drive and I heard Mom invite her in for coffee. Ugh. I'd been looking forward to a nap. The three of us formed a sluggish parade to the house. Mom shuffled straight to the big, overstuffed chair. I guessed that meant I was making coffee and began to head toward the kitchen, but Clair grabbed my shoulders and directed me to the living room. "I'll get it."

"Thank you." I aimed my tired body for the sofa and kicked off my shoes. Within seconds, I was stretched out with a pillow tucked under my head.

Clair called as she left the room. "We could all use a pick-me-up. Coffee will be ready in a few minutes."

Mom leaned her head back and stared into space. I closed my eyes. The tinkling of glass and sounds of gushing water floated in from the kitchen. Before long, Clair arrived with two cups of coffee. She handed one to Mom and the other to me. I breathed out my thanks and balanced the cup while arranging myself at an angle where I could drink it without spilling. Clair returned to the kitchen for her own.

When I'd finally managed to get comfortable, a melodic chime sounded.

Mom glanced at me. "I'll never get used to that new doorbell." She began unfolding her legs and pulling herself from the deep cushions of the chair.

I put up a hand. "Don't get up." I set my cup on the floor and began my own struggle from the couch.

"Lib, stay where you are." Clair set her coffee on the end table. "I'll get rid of whoever it is. You've been through enough."

She trotted to the front door and returned a moment later followed by Pastor Prescott. Mom stood. I resumed my struggle to obtain a sitting position.

The pastor held up his hands. "Please ladies, just sit. No need to be formal with me." He quickly lowered himself into a side chair. "I'm fine right here."

My mother hesitantly took her seat. "How nice of you to stop by, Pastor. Can I get you a cup of coffee?" With that she was on her feet again and on her way to the kitchen. Clair blocked her path.

"Katherine, sit down. I'll get it."

Pastor Prescott waved her away. "No coffee for me. I'm here to offer encouragement and to discover what the church may do for you."

"That's so kind of you, Pastor. We're doing fine." Mom put on her brightest smile and settled back into her chair.

Lord, forgive my mother for fibbing. She was obviously exhausted and not fine.

Pastor Prescott informed us of meals organized by the church ladies and of the prayers the prayer team offered on our behalf. I'm not sure my mother felt completely comfortable with the helpfulness of the church. These were all the duties that had been in her charge for as long as I could remember.

Conversation slowed and Clair was quick to fill the void. "Katherine, I've been wondering. How did Peggy find you at the library?"

Mom glanced toward Clair. "A very good question. Imagine my surprise when Peggy described being in Twin Fawn several times before this visit. She'd been tracking me and had even been in my house." Mom directed her gaze at me. "That would be your house, Liberty. Peggy wasn't aware I'd sold it to you."

I shook my head. "How did she even know to come to Twin Fawn?"

My mother shrugged. "That is something I don't know. I'd been careful not to let anyone in Evelynton know where I'd moved." She looked at me. "And your grandparents were adamant that people didn't need to know my business. I guess that was a hint they'd always been aware I had a secret."

Mom paused to sip her coffee. "Over the years, I suppose they let their guard down and mistakenly mentioned it to someone. Anyway, once Peggy had that information she came here and tracked me down."

I glanced at Clair at the same moment she pressed her lips together and narrowed her eyes at me. Had we told Peggy we were from Twin Fawn? Had we directed a mentally disturbed woman to my mother's home?

I returned attention to my mother. Her smile had brightened as she spoke. "During our conversation in the library, Peggy complimented our little town. She seemed impressed that everyone she met was so friendly and willing to tell her anything she wanted to know."

The pastor inhaled. "Oh my. I must have been one of those helpful people. I remember a nice lady visited the church one day when I was in the office. She asked about Katherine Baron. Of course, I recognized the name because of our meetings, and even told her your married name. The woman said she wanted to surprise an old friend."

He raised both hands and smiled. "Well, that sounded like a wonderful idea. I thought you would enjoy the visit." He turned his attention to Clair and me. "We had a nice chat and I told her what a treasure Katherine had always been. I raved about her volunteer work and her contribution to our thriving library."

The pastor breathed a sigh and leaned forward with elbows on his knees. "I should have known better. I'm so sorry if I contributed to your trouble."

Mom waved a hand. "Well, it certainly was a surprise

to see her walking into the library with a gun in her hand. But don't give it another thought. That woman would have found me eventually, and I'm glad she did. Now she will begin healing from the damage caused by holding on to her anger. Imagine the harm it has done."

I clenched my teeth. I'd thought I would never speak of it again. But now I found I needed all the details. "Peggy's anger was evident when we met her. But I never thought she would have been capable of bringing a weapon to Twin Fawn."

"Her feelings had been festering. I suspect Peggy had a crush on Bernie from the beginning. After all, why would she have listened to him when he ordered everyone to protect my identity? I should have recognized it at the time. But being so self-centered, I'm not sure it would have made any difference."

Mom stared out the window and ran her fingers through her hair for a moment. "Bernie was in prison. Eddie and Gary had left town. Just think about it. Peggy had only Joan to share the secret with. And after Joan's death, there was no one. She probably felt so alone and abandoned. Anger and blame continued to build up against me."

Mom planted both feet on the floor. "I'll be sure to visit her while she's in jail and apologize again. Maybe I can help her find peace."

The pastor nodded. "You are a good woman. I'm sure your experience these past years help you understand her pain."

"I'm so glad there are no more secrets. The truth sets us all free."

My mother escorted the pastor to the door and waved as he left. This time, when she turned to Clair and me, her smile stretched all the way across her face. "Well girls, let's get back to enjoying the peace and quiet of Twin Fawn."

~~~

It had been several peaceful weeks since the incident at the library. The leaves were off the trees, but the sun shone brightly giving the promise of an unseasonably warm afternoon. A light jacket was all I needed as I walked to work. I'd left home early, leaving plenty of time to enjoy Bird Song Park. I noticed other citizens took advantage of the mild weather to enjoy their morning walk as well. From my place on the park bench, I enjoyed people watching. Happy families. Peaceful lives.

Who would have guessed my mother had been keeping secret guilt for so many years. Now the mask had been ripped off, and she was free. I closed my eyes for a moment and took a deep breath. "Thank you, Lord, that life is back to normal."

A squeal caused my heart to thump until I saw my neighbor, Kessie Baker, passing. The wheels of her personal shopping cart had produced the annoying squeak for as long as I could remember. Kessie Baker, true to her name, was a great cook. She had been kind to my mother and me, bringing us fresh baked cinnamon rolls on occasion.

"Good morning, Kessie. You're out early."

"I like to get my grocery shopping done in the morning. Isn't it a glorious day?"

I nodded my agreement. "How's Carson?"

"Oh, my husband is in his glory. So happy the weather is still mild enough to get in another round of golf."

She waddled past and I called after her. "Have a good day."

"Oh, I plan to." Kessie laughed. It was a loud laugh. So much that I thought I must have missed something. Private joke?

I swiveled in my seat and watched her as she travelled down the next block, still wondering about Kessie's laugh. Likely none of my business. Could that sweet little woman, who baked goodies for the neighborhood, have a secret life? Not likely.

More neighbors passed Kessie, coming in my direction. Ron and Linda Charrigan. I swiveled back to the front as they passed. Linda smiled, but quickly turned her eyes to the sidewalk ahead. Probably in a hurry. What had happened to Ron? He limped and had difficulty keeping up with her. She should slow down a bit.

I wanted to inquire about his health, but she walked quickly out of earshot and I hesitated to detain him. The couple reached the end of the block and I was alone in the park.

I glanced at the sky, wondering why the light had dimmed. Clouds partially concealed the sun. Had the birds stopped singing? My mood had dimmed also as I wondered how many families in this sweet small town harbored dark secrets?

Silly me. My imagination running wild. Not everyone wore a mask to hide their true selves. Kessie Baker had thought of something funny as she passed me. Ron and Linda were obviously late for an appointment, and he twisted his ankle or maybe had a leg cramp.

Guess I'd been watching too much crime TV. What could be hidden behind the closed doors of Twin Fawn? I mean other than last decade's clothing styles and canned goods marked past their sell-by date.

The End

Mystery writer Lynne Waite Chapman loves people, small towns and mystery. She is the author of the four book <u>Evelynton Murder Series,</u> beginning with award winning mystery novel <u>Heart Strings</u>.

She began her writing career with fifteen years of providing weekly nonfiction content for the BellaOnline.com Hair site, drawing on thirty plus years of experience in cosmetology. Retiring the Hair site, she spent fifteen years writing weekly nonfiction content for Christian Living at BellaOnline.com and published a devotional study of the women of the Bible, <u>A Walk With Eve.</u>

Lynne now directs her efforts toward mysteries with an inspirational message.

Heart Strings
https://www.amazon.com/dp/1944203621

Heart Beat
https://www.amazon.com/dp/1946939250

Murderous Heart
https://www.amazon.com/dp/1792872259

Caffeinated Murder
https://www.amazon.com/gp/product/B087FVZGQC

Amazon Author Page

https://amazon.com/author/lwchapman

Web site

https://www.lynnechapman.com

www.ingramcontent.com/pod-product-compliance
Lightning Source LLC
LaVergne TN
LVHW010320070526
838199LV00065B/5612